YOU are being

CONSUMED

by The

REINCARNATION

KOURTNEA HOGAN

SOUL

TRAP

ISBN: 978-1-68510-053-7 (sc)
ISBN: 978-1-68510-054-4 (ebook)

First printing edition: July 29, 2022
Printed by Bizarro Pulp Press in the United States of America.
Cover Design and Layout: Don Noble
Edited by Nick Day
Proofreading and Interior Layout by Scarlett R. Algee

Bizarro Pulp Press, an imprint of JournalStone Publishing
3205 Sassafras Trail
Carbondale, Illinois 62901

Bizarro Pulp Press books may be ordered through booksellers or by contacting:

JournalStone | www.journalstone.com

CONSUME

CHAPTER 1

TEGAN PINCHED AND PULLED at the flab of skin that fell over the band of her underwear. *"It's baby fat,"* her mother's words echoed through her mind. She was thirteen; not a baby anymore. She'd been practicing starving herself for the past few weeks and had seen a little bit of progress, but it wasn't quick enough.

The kids at school didn't really tease her, but she knew they could see every roll and stretch mark through her clothing. Maybe they whispered about it. Then again, she wasn't important enough for that.

It wasn't that people hated her, though she made herself throw up from worrying they did, it was just they didn't care about her. It was almost worse, really. It was her own fault though. She was so quiet. She spoke when prodded, but her hands shook, and her voice always caught in her throat.

She pulled on her school clothes, noticing how the shirt and blue jeans fit her, making her look wider.

Being invisible did have its advantages though. She could watch people. She could watch Rileigh Banister. She could watch the sun rays turn her hair into thin tendrils of gold. Could watch it shimmer in the light as it kissed her shoulders, thin and prominent beneath the white shirt that clung to her thin frame.

"Tegan."

Tegan was snapped back into reality at the mention of her name. Her cheeks burned at the thought of someone catching her staring at Rileigh, but Jordan Huckleberry had already turned his attention back to his friends, leaving her with a stack of papers to pass down the line.

Busy work. That's all Mr. Scott gave them to do in biology. She couldn't remember a single time he'd ever actually taught them anything. She was pretty sure she was one of the only people who read the sections of the book he assigned, but everyone had a passing grade anyway. Tegan imagined if you just scribbled something down he'd count it right, but that shit wasn't going to fly in high school, and she wanted to get ahead.

She passed the papers to the right and received a reflexive, "Thanks," from Bailey Morriss. He might have even smiled at her out of politeness, but she was already cracking open the biology book with a picture of a man holding a surfboard on the cover. What that had to do with biology she wasn't totally sure.

A strand of her hair, long and dark, slid onto the page. She stared at it out of the corner of her eye for a few seconds. It was dark enough to always appear slightly greasy, even after she'd just washed it. It didn't glitter in the sunlight shining through the windows like Rileigh's did. It remained as flat and lifeless as it did outside of the sun's warmth.

She pulled a hair tie off her wrist and slicked her hair back into a sloppy bun. Hair snaked out of the band and tickled her neck. Bailey was watching her. She let the pieces lay against her skin and tried to make it look as though she was concentrating on her work.

He was still looking. What was he staring at? What was wrong with her? She wanted to look him in the eye, to ask what he wanted, but she couldn't bring herself to look at him. Her skin burned where his eyes lingered.

She pushed her chair back a little too loudly and approached Mr. Scott's desk. He was watching some video on YouTube. From where she was standing it didn't look very school appropriate, but she didn't care.

"What's up?" he asked without looking away from the screen. The unnatural light touched all the lines on his face, giving him a gaunt, sickly appearance. *Maybe he came in drunk again today.*

"Can I use the restroom, please?"

"I don't know, can you?" His smile was all teeth.

Tegan closed her eyes before she could roll them. She was tired of being at the front of the room and having everyone's eyes on her. "May I—"

"I'm just joshin' ya." He wrenched open the top left drawer and dropped the pack of pink passes on the desk.

He held the pass out to her, but jerked it out of her reach just as her fingertips brushed its edges. Her face burned and her hands shook. She wondered if he noticed. The stares of everyone in the room burned into her back.

Mr. Scott laughed and held it out again. He didn't pull it away this time.

"Thank you." She turned quickly.

"Hey, Tegan."

She stopped and looked back in his direction, but not at him. "Mr. Scott?"

"You have a lovely voice. You should talk more."

She didn't know what to say to this, so she simply nodded and watched her feet reach the door. Tegan closed it quietly and leaned against the cold, concrete blocks. She looked in through the small window in the door. No one was watching her. Bailey had taken his phone out and was texting beneath the table.

She climbed the stairs up to the second story and ducked inside the bathroom. No one ever used the bathroom by the staircase; mostly because it had an odd smell. Someone had dumped a perfume bottle all over the floor at the beginning of the semester and the scent of vanilla and alcohol still lingered.

Tegan locked the door from the inside just to be safe. She hung her messenger bag on the coat hook and marched into the handicap stall. She made a small pillow of toilet paper in front of the toilet to kneel upon. She thrust her finger down her throat and dry heaved. She dug further back, scratching her tonsils. She spat out a little bit of blood, but nothing else.

She leaned away from the toilet and pinched her stomach. Her fingernails dug deep into her skin through her t-shirt. Maybe she would make herself bleed again.

Someone pulled on the door.

Tegan froze.

Silence.

Her shoulders were hiked up by her ears. She tried to breathe.

The person knocked. "Hello?" A man's voice.

"Fuck," Tegan whispered. She lifted herself off the floor and clambered to shove the toilet paper into the bowl.

"Hello?" he asked again.

Tegan could hear keys jangling through the door. "Just a minute!" She spat out another wad of blood and flushed the toilet. She ripped her messenger bag off the hook and reached to open the door, but it swung in on her before her fingers were fully wrapped around the handle.

The janitor pushed his head through the crack. Concern brought out the lines on his face. "Everything ok in here?"

"Yes. Sorry. I felt sick." She wanted to push through the door, but she didn't want to brush past him. There was a knot in her stomach like a fist. Maybe she'd be able to throw up now.

"You can't lock the door, hun."

Hun. The word stung. She didn't want to be coddled, didn't want whatever this attention was.

"Yeah. I know. I'm sorry."

The janitor nodded and opened the door a little wider. Tegan seized her opportunity and squeezed through the crack.

"It's ok. Do you need to go to the nurse?" he called.

She was already halfway down the staircase. "No thank you." She didn't yell. If he heard it, he heard it, and if he didn't, she didn't really care. She heard him call after her again, but she merely sped up.

A few people looked as she came back into the room. The fist in her stomach tightened. She wished she hadn't left the restroom.

But the gazes didn't linger for too long, and everyone had forgotten about her again by the time she slid back into her seat. Bailey was wrapped up in conversation with the boy in front of him, so she didn't have to worry about him either.

The fist released a little, and soon enough, she was caught up in her bookwork and the things that caused her anxiety melted into the background.

CHAPTER 2

TEGAN HAD HAD FRIENDS once. Not that long ago really. But when her mom died, suddenly her father dragged her two states away.

She was terrible at keeping in touch. The feeling she was a burden on others always took up residence in the back of her mind.

Besides, it was too much for her father. That's why he'd dragged them away from their home. Everything reminded him of her mom. Tegan felt the same at first, so she didn't really complain.

She held onto the thought that she might be able to reconnect with her friends once her dad got better. But it had been a year since the move and a few months since she'd gotten a phone call.

Her dad wasn't much of a talker— wasn't much of a crier either. They were similar in that aspect. If she needed to talk to someone she would talk to her cat, Stella. And if she needed a little human interaction, she would make popcorn and watch the game show channel with her dad.

The kids at school weren't mean to her. They barely paid her any attention, but when they did, they were polite.

And maybe if she didn't avoid eye contact with a smile and nod when asked questions instead of trying to further a conversation, she could make some friends.

But, as it were, she sat at her lunch table alone. Well, not totally alone. There were other people there, but they didn't really talk to one another. Every once in a while, she'd trade something off her tray with another quiet girl, Amelia, but that was as far as the interactions went.

Amelia had her nose shoved in some *Fear Street* book before Tegan had even sat down. There was another one next to her tray. She brought her pizza up to her mouth every few minutes, her eyes never leaving the page.

Tegan dabbed the extra grease off her own square pizza with a napkin. Eating pizza at lunch everyday probably didn't help her pudgy stomach, but it was the only edible food the cafeteria offered, and she'd limited herself to only salad at home.

There weren't really any cliques at Polk Middle School. People hung out with their friends. There wasn't some kind of invisible line between the orchestra kids and the cheerleaders or anything.

She liked that. If she hated herself less, and actually tried to put herself out there, she felt like she'd be accepted.

The boys at the table behind her were being loud. She wished she could disappear into a book like Amelia, but she wasn't much of a reader. That would at least keep the noise from bothering her too much.

"What the fuck did you just say?" one of the boys yelled. The metal legs of his chair screeched as he jumped up.

Amelia looked up from her book but didn't put it down.

Tegan turned to watch. Everyone's attention was on the table behind her.

"You heard what I fucking said. If I see you around Chrissy again, you're dead."

Mr. Scott and Mrs. Oliver finally turned their attention to the table.

Mrs. Oliver moved across the room immediately. She was a short woman who looked like a toad, so quick for her wasn't saying too much.

Tegan didn't recognize the boys, and didn't know who Chrissy was, but she'd guess the girl had a type. Both boys were tall and thin with tanned skin and shaggy blond hair. If you'd have told her they were brothers, she would have believed it.

Mr. Scott was still posted up against the far wall, eyeing the boys. He wouldn't step in until they started throwing fists. He didn't want to ruin his reputation as the "cool teacher."

Tegan thought she should get out of the way, but the boy behind her had slammed his chair into hers, trapping her.

And if she was trapped, she might as well watch.

The tension in the room was electric as the boys stared each other down, neither budging. But Mrs. Oliver was closing in now, nearly within arm's reach of the boy furthest from Tegan.

He noticed this, and in one swift motion, grabbed his tray and flung it at the other boy, yelling, "Bitch!"

The boy's reflexes were too quick, and the hard plastic caught his fingers as he pushed it behind him and onto Tegan.

The boy wasn't unscathed – mashed potatoes were dripping down the front of him. But Tegan got the brunt of it.

Chocolate milk streamed down her hair and onto her face. The rest of the warm mashed potatoes and gravy had splattered across the front of her white shirt. A fruit cup dripped in her lap, soaking through her pants and underwear.

That creeping cold is what snapped her out of her shock.

Mr. Scott had already made his way across the cafeteria and was between the two boys, who, as far as Tegan knew, hadn't really gotten the opportunity to punch each other.

She was rushing into the bathroom before she really knew she was moving.

A clump of mashed potatoes slid off her shoulder and onto the floor. She turned the sink water on as hot as it would go and forced her head under the faucet, her breasts squishing against the porcelain. It might have been painful if she could feel anything besides embarrassment. She couldn't stop her hands from shaking.

She wanted to rip her stained shirt off, wanted to throw away her clothes and sink into the ground. But instead, she freed her head from its confinement and wet a paper towel to scrub at her shirt and pants. Her wet hair slapped against her back and warm water cascaded onto her pants.

Footsteps.

No. She didn't want to deal with anybody's sympathies, or worse, their laughter. She flung herself into the first stall, but someone snaked their fingers in before she could close it.

Rileigh pushed through. The fluorescent light made her hair shimmer.

"Hey," she said, as if she was talking to a wild animal. "You ok?"

Tegan opened her mouth to speak, but a lump rose in her throat, and the tears she'd been holding back ran down her cheeks.

Rileigh instinctively wrapped her arms around Tegan and pulled her close. She stroked Tegan's hair. "Shhh, it's ok."

"Everyone is laughing at me."

They must all really be getting a kick out of it. Suddenly, Tegan was aware that Rileigh's hands barely wrapped completely around her.

"I don't think anyone noticed you really. Or if they did, they've forgotten it already. One of the boys punched Mr. Scott in the mouth." Rileigh pulled back and clasped Tegan's face in her hands. They were warm and soft and smelled vaguely like honeysuckle. "Besides, if they were laughing, fuck 'em. They're assholes for it."

Tegan had never expected Rileigh to curse, and she giggled. Rileigh smiled and wiped the tears from Tegan's face.

"Thanks." Tegan pulled away to compose herself.

Rileigh wiped her hands on her jeans. "Want me to grab a teacher and have them go to the office to call your mom?"

Tegan bristled at the assumption that her mom would pick her up, but it faded quickly. "Um, my dad actually."

The bell rang, and the room filled with the sound of chairs scraping and people filing out of the cafeteria.

"Fuck," Tegan mumbled.

"It's ok." Rileigh motioned to the door. "I'll tell one of the teachers, and then, I'll walk you, ok?"

Before Tegan could answer, Rileigh was already out of the stall.

Water dripped down Tegan's back. She opened the stall door and stared at her reflection. Her skin was flushed. She looked pathetic. But Rileigh was right, there was nothing to be embarrassed about. She'd done nothing wrong. So why was her chest so tight?

Rileigh entered the room with the principal right behind. Tegan blinked back at them. A new wave of embarrassment hit, but it subsided as soon as Rileigh took Tegan's hand in hers.

Tegan looked at the interlocked fingers, stayed focused on them, until they were in the office. She hadn't been touched in so long, not since she'd held her father's hand during the funeral. She worried about her palms sweating.

"All right, I'll write you a pass to go back to class," called Principal Erikson over her shoulder. Tegan looked up.

"Thank you," Rileigh answered. Principal Erikson scribbled on the pad and slid the pass across the secretary's desk. The secretary was already on the phone with Tegan's father.

Rileigh released Tegan's hand and smiled, gripping her shoulders. "I hope you feel better. See you tomorrow, Tegan."

Tegan watched Rileigh's golden hair sway with her steps until she was no longer in sight.

"You can sit down, honey." The secretary spoke slowly and softly as though addressing a much younger child.

It took Tegan's dad nearly an hour to get there, them living in the country and all. But Tegan was too busy basking in the afterglow of being cared for by Rileigh (or being cared for at all—who knew?) to really mind.

Her father was worried, but he didn't know what to say, didn't know how to comfort her. So, they rode home in silence.

CHAPTER 3

TEGAN POURED EXTRA BUBBLES into the bathtub and ran a bit more hot water.

The water was dangerously close to the lip of the tub, but Tegan stopped it before it could overflow.

The bubbles covered her whole body, which is what she wanted. She couldn't stand the sight of herself. If she was covered, she could pretend that she was thin and pretty. That she was worthy of attention.

She'd been in the tub for over an hour, cycling through warm and cold water, trying to stay stuck in the moment where Rileigh held her. She'd told herself that she didn't like physical contact, but now that she'd really had some she wanted more.

Her father knocked on the door. Tegan shifted in the tub and water sloshed over the side and onto the floor.

"Dinner's ready." Her father's voice boomed from behind the door.

"Thanks."

A pause, but he didn't leave.

"Are you ok in there?"

"I'm fine." Her response sounded barbed, though she didn't mean it to be. "Thanks, Dad."

She flipped the switch with her big toe. The water gurgled down the drain, leaving trails of bubbles clinging to the tub and her skin. She shifted and released the water that had been trapped between her and the tub. The noise made her stomach tighten. Her fat thighs and ass had trapped the stream that quickly disappeared down the drain.

She turned the hot water knob over as far as it would go and turned the shower on.

A brief burst of cold water struck her chest. She gritted her teeth, feeling the skin around her temples tighten.

The water had been hot enough to turn her skin red, but she'd already used most of the hot water and she was covered in goosebumps by the time she got out.

She caught a glimpse of her naked body in the mirror as she dried off and side-stepped away from her imperfections.

No. You really need to take a look at yourself.

She wrapped her hair and stepped back into the mirror's view. She guessed she didn't look awful from the front, but when she turned to the side, she could see her pudge threatening to fall onto the tops of her thighs.

Her ears burned beneath the towel.

Her stomach growled, and she seized a chunk of her skin and squeezed until little blood droplets crested beneath her fingernails.

She quickly pulled on the baggy night clothes that hid her frame.

She walked to her room, patting the ends of her hair. Her wet feet left little indents in the white carpet. There was a yellow stain in front of her door that you wouldn't notice unless you were looking for it, that was born earlier in the year from Tegan dropping a bowl of mac 'n cheese. She'd accidently stepped in it. She could never forget the wet feeling between her toes, and she avoided the spot religiously.

She flopped down on her bed and rubbed the paisley comforter absentmindedly.

The walls were a dull pink that she hated. It had once belonged to a little girl obsessed with ballerinas. Both of her parents were still alive.

Her dad's heavy footsteps lurched up the stairs.

"Tegan? Baby, you hungry?"

"No."

He stopped a few feet away from her doorway.

Her pulse echoed in her ears. She didn't want to have a heart-to-heart. Not with him anyway. She closed her eyes and pictured Rileigh's golden hair catching the light.

"I love you, kid."

"Love you too."

His footsteps faded.

Tegan folded her hands on her stomach (the upper part, the small part) and closed her eyes. The light above her bed burned through her eyelids and yellow circles danced in the darkness. She thought of Rileigh, and how she was the vision of perfection. People liked Rileigh. They made an effort to talk to her, and she genuinely cherished every interaction.

Her skin was beautiful, not milky like hers, but full of a natural glow that burned through in the summer, offsetting her pale hair.

Her eyes were green in some light and blue in others. Tegan liked them better green.

She moved her hand higher, to the hollow where her ribs separated. Her heartbeat fluttered against her fingers.

She imagined what Rileigh's heartbeat felt like. She should have paid more attention to the details when she was being held. She squeezed her eyes shut and imagined their bodies pressed together, free of clothing and sexless.

Of Rileigh's stomach pressing against Tegan's, flattening it—flattening all of her until they were one being with shining gold hair and sun kissed skin.

She squeezed her eyes tighter, her vision black and red. Her body was tight—aching for some kind of release.

Click

She jolted up and opened her eyes. Stars danced in the blackness and she swayed from the head rush.

"You fell asleep," her father said before slinking to his room.

Her skin was hot and damp. She lay in the darkness for some time, forcing herself not to close her eyes and get lost again.

CHAPTER 4

RILEIGH WAS RIGHT. NO one noticed what happened to Tegan. Or at least no one paid any special attention to her.

She slid into her seat at the back of Mrs. Jenner's class. She wished the bell would ring so that she could put her headphones in and do her busy work. Mrs. Jenner was pretty laid back and history came easy to Tegan anyway.

She kept her eyes down, flipping through her playlist, trying to find a song, as the rest of the class filtered in.

Someone placed their hand on her shoulder as the other hand daintily slid books onto the desk beside her. Rileigh's smiling face slid into view. Tegan relaxed her shoulders. Was Riliegh smiling at her? Really?

"Hey, girl. How are you?"

"Oh. Uh. Hey. I'm fine." Tegan had to clear her throat. She wasn't so used to using her voice.

Rileigh slid into the seat beside Tegan and brushed her long hair off her shoulders.

"Ugh, I'm so ready for the day to be over. Are you doing anything fun this weekend?"

Tegan blinked.

Rileigh's laughter filled the room, sounding like tinkling bells. "Well?"

"I'm sorry."

"No need to be. You're really quiet, huh?"

"Yeah." Tegan looked down at her books.

"I like that. You seem like you'd be a good listener." Rileigh gripped Tegan's knee. "And they make the best friends."

The bell splitting the brief silence was distraction enough from Tegan's hot face.

Rileigh turned forward, her hair swinging against her back. Tegan wondered how it felt, if it tickled or felt like a loving touch.

Mrs. Jenner waved her hands to get the class's attention. Tegan faced her direction, but was still sizing up Rileigh in her peripheral vision.

This is a "Carrie" scenario. The popular kids are all going to torment me for no fucking reason. Because I'm different.

Mrs. Jenner was setting up a PowerPoint.

At least I'll get to kill them all.

She pulled out her history notebook.

"Oh man, you have a whole notebook for each class?" Rileigh stared in wonder. "You're so put together."

Tegan smiled through tight lips, careful not to make eye contact.

Her stomach stayed locked in a tight ball for the entirety of the class. She was conscious of every slight movement, every breath. She didn't want to draw any more attention to herself, didn't want to experience the teasing (or worse, pity) that was right around the corner.

She concentrated on making herself as small as possible and couldn't focus on anything Mrs. Jenner was saying. She felt as though she was personally betraying her favorite teacher. The tall, thin-faced woman was still talking about the 1970's, one of Tegan's favorite eras, clapping her hands together at the conclusion.

"All right, guys, we're almost out of time here," she said. The students immediately began to shove their supplies into their backpacks.

Tegan shot a glance at the clock, her neck stiff from sitting so still. Only five minutes until the bell would ring. She was surprised the other students had waited so long to start packing up; but then again, everyone loved Mrs. Jenner and her genuine love for history.

Mrs. Jenner held up her hands. "You can keep packing up but pay attention, ok? Remember how I told you that you'd have a big project to do before the end of the semester?" The class groaned in response. Mrs. Jenner smiled. "Come on now, guys, it isn't that bad. You will be split up into groups of two, and each of you will cover an era that we've discussed in class up to the 70's. I need you to make a PowerPoint to refresh the class including at least two potential test questions the class will answer together. And just like usual, I'll let you pick your partners, so go ahead and do that for me, please."

There wasn't much movement, as nearly everyone was already seated next to their friends, but a few people near the front of the room shuffled seats.

Rileigh leaned over to Tegan. Her hair brushed against Tegan's arm.

A shiver ran through her body that morphed to a warmth she'd never felt.

"So, we're gonna be partners, right?"

"Sure. If you want." Tegan was surprised at how little she stuttered this time.

Rileigh smiled, revealing perfectly straight, white teeth. "Aren't you really good at history?"

"Yeah, I guess so." *How did she know that?*

As if she could read Tegan's thoughts, Rileigh said, "You always get to choose your topic and stuff."

"Are we all settled?" Mrs. Jenner clapped her hands again. The room was still electric with the giggles and whispers of students. "All right, per usual, the student with the highest grade gets to pick their era first, and that would be Tegan."

The bell saved Tegan from the embarrassment of having the class turn around to stare at her.

"Oh, dang it," sighed Mrs. Jenner and looked to the clock as though not believing time could have possibly passed. "Guys!" She tried to project out to the hall where a good portion of the students already were. "I'll see you again on Thursday, so think about the top three decades you would like to cover!" She looked back at the students that remained. "You think they heard me?"

"Probably not," said Rileigh, with a smirk. "You can't hear anything in the hall."

The sound of students laughing, yelling across to one another, and running to use the bathroom before the bell rang infiltrated the room.

Mrs. Jenner laughed. "Touché." She went to her station outside of her door to monitor the chaos.

Tegan placed everything carefully in her bag. Her next class was only two doors away. And maybe Rileigh would abandon her if she was slow enough. She didn't really want Rileigh to leave her behind, but the sense that the attention was all some sick joke had burrowed deep into her mind. It made her feel bad to think that way of Rileigh, and she wished she could stop, but she knew how awful she truly was, and she knew Rileigh had to see it too.

But Rileigh hadn't left. She pulled her teal bag up over one shoulder and watched Tegan patiently.

"Any idea of what decade you want to do?"

Tegan bent forward so her hair covered her face. "I was thinking the 1970's. Unless you would rather do something else."

"That's fine with me. We can talk about Vietnam and stuff."

"Yeah."

"Hey, do you wanna come over this weekend and do it? You can stay the night."

Tegan whipped around to face Rileigh. Her bag slammed to the ground.

Rileigh finally looked taken aback by Tegan. "I mean, if you don't want to that's cool too."

"No, no. I want to. I'm sorry. I'm just...not good with people. Not used to someone wanting to spend time with me."

A warmth spread through Rileigh's eyes and Tegan wanted to hold her close and tell her that she was sorry for making her feel bad, that she wasn't worth the trouble. The thought of them melting together blinked through her mind and her nipples hardened. She covered her chest, her face growing hot.

"Tegan, I really would like to get to know you. I'm not doing this out of pity or anything, ok? I like making new friends, and I've always thought you were so cool and smart."

Tegan didn't know if she was going to laugh or throw up. "Me?"

"Yeah. I mean, you have the highest grade in nearly every class we're in. Everyone always talks about how smart you are."

People talk about me? I exist when I'm not around?

"Thank you. But I'm not cool. At all. You're the cool one."

Rileigh rolled her eyes. "Yeah right. People talk to me because I never shut up. But you don't care if people talk to you. You do your own thing. It's really cool. I feel kind of special that you talk to me at all."

All the hair on Tegan's arms stood up. She tried to block the thought of their naked bodies pressing into each other, becoming one another, out of her mind. Her stomach knotted, knowing that enjoying these thoughts was wrong. She was wrong.

The warning bell didn't stop the thoughts, but it did make Rileigh look away from her.

Mrs. Jenner popped her head back into her room. "Girls, that was the warning. Come on."

"Sorry, Mrs. Jenner." Rileigh walked to the door. She turned over her shoulder and waved at Tegan. "See you tomorrow, Tegan." She disappeared through the doorway.

Tegan nearly tripped over her bag trying to follow.

CHAPTER 5

"WELL, OF COURSE YOU can go." Her dad looked the happiest she'd seen him in a long time. "A slumber party." His smile touched his eyes for the first time in ages.

He reached across the dinner table and rubbed Tegan's arm. She would have just gone to Rileigh's right after school, but Fridays were the only night her dad tore himself away from the television and the two had dinner together. Afterwards, they would watch a movie or play a game. Tegan enjoyed them sometimes, but it made her happy to make her dad happy, so she played along as much as possible.

"What are we playing tonight?" Tegan picked at the salad on her plate. Her dad had made hamburgers, but it wasn't worth the fat or the calories. Over the past week she'd eaten so little that sometimes her body would get unbearably warm, and she felt like she was either going to throw up or pass out. She took that as a sign that it was working.

Her dad spoke through a mouthful of burger. "Oh, I don't know, kid. Whatever you want to play. Or we can watch a movie. It doesn't matter to me." Grease dripped from his mouth and into his beard. A few droplets dotted the tablecloth.

Tegan picked a sliver of carrot out of the salad and put it in her mouth. She chewed it slowly, rolling it between her teeth, putting pressure on it until it snapped. "I don't care, Dad. Whatever you want."

He wiped the grease from his beard with a napkin. "Do you want to play The Game of Life?"

It was his favorite game, but the first time they'd played it after her mother had died, he'd broken down in tears about halfway through. Tegan had refused to play the last few times he'd asked, getting irate and stomping up the stairs the most recent time.

"Yeah. We haven't played that in forever."

She expected some kind of sadness to take over him again, the kind of sadness that hung all around him while he sulked in his recliner. But it didn't. He beamed at her, his mouth full of food, and did a little dance in his seat.

Tegan snorted and the two began to giggle. Her dad hid his face behind a napkin and Tegan covered her mouth with her hands. They finally quieted but laughed even harder than before when their eyes met.

Her dad rose from the table, still chuckling, and grabbed the game from the bookcase in the corner of the dining room. Tegan cleaned the table, dumping the rest of her food into the trash and covering it with a napkin.

***

Her dad's Subaru rocked back and forth down the dirt road. Every so often a rock would *ping!* against the body.

Tegan thought she lived in the middle of nowhere, but it was nowhere close to the distance of Rileigh's house. She felt like they'd been driving for forever and she still couldn't even see a hint of the house. If she wasn't so nervous, she wouldn't have minded. They were surrounded by fields of deep green foliage. In the distance was a wall of trees, full and welcoming. Tegan wished she could run through the fields and into the trees. Into the nothingness.

"Your destination will be on the left in two miles," the GPS advised.

Tegan turned her attention back to the road.

"Is that it?" Her dad pointed over the steering wheel.

In the distance loomed a massive farmhouse. A large, red barn sat to the side. Tegan wondered what kind of animals they kept. Her excitement grew even more when she saw the pool in the backyard.

By the time they pulled into the driveway, Rileigh and her parents were standing outside. Rileigh bounded off the wraparound porch and up to the car.

She took Tegan's bag from her hands. "I'll get that."

"Oh, you don't have to."

"I wouldn't be a good host if I didn't."

Her parents—a beautiful blonde, tanned couple—descended the steps. Rileigh's dad reached out and shook Tegan's dad's hand.

"Hey, how are ya?"

"Doing good, thanks." Tegan's dad looked as uncomfortable as she normally felt. She understood where she got her people skills.

"You girls go ahead inside," Rileigh's dad called, waving them away. "We're just gonna talk for a sec."

But Rileigh was already pushing through the screen door. The smell of honeysuckle greeted her at the doorway. Tegan stopped to admire the mudroom, which housed three tiny benches with each member's name stenciled on and a coat hook above it. The paint on the walls was cracked (in a stylish farmhouse way) and a beautiful Robin's egg blue. It was the kind of house you saw in magazines. A giant ornate mirror hung above a small table that held up a vase full of wildflowers.

"Come on, my room's up here." Rileigh was already halfway up the stairs.

Tegan walked as softly as she could, trying not to make heavy footsteps.

The floor upstairs was all hardwood. It looked as though it had been worn down on purpose.

Rileigh pushed into the bedroom at the end of the hall. "In here."

Tegan quickened her pace.

The room was big and beautiful. Tegan marveled at all the little trinkets suspended by decorative hooks on the walls. A colorful chandelier caught the light from a big bay window and dotted the room in pinks, yellows, blues, and purples. A fuzzy, white rug rested beneath the four- poster bed.

Rileigh tossed Tegan's bag onto a green armchair that was nestled between two white bookcases filled with books, games, and knick-knacks before opening the top drawer of her dresser.

"You brought your swimsuit, right?"

Tegan blushed and instinctively covered her stomach. "Yeah."

Rileigh pulled out a pink and white one piece. "Let's go swimming." She unbuttoned her pants.

Tegan coughed and turned to the bookcases. "Shouldn't we get started on the project?"

"We only have a few more hours of sunshine. You'll be here all night. Let's have fun first." She shimmied out of her pants.

Tegan heard them hit the floor. She shuffled toward the chair, focused on the fabric, even when she heard Rileigh's pants hit the ground.

"I'll go change in the bathroom."

"Don't be silly. We're girls. You can change in here."

Tears threatened to spill down Tegan's cheeks. She was already going to be embarrassed to be seen in the skin-tight bathing suit. She certainly didn't want Rileigh to see her naked. And she didn't want to see Rileigh's body either. She'd be too tempted to touch it. Too tempted to feel her warmth, to try to melt together with her.

She snatched the bag off the chair and went into the hall in what felt like one swift motion.

"Bathroom is right across the hall!" Rileigh's voice spilled after her.

Tegan closed the bathroom door harder than she'd intended. Her sweaty hands slid off the lock the first few times she reached for it.

The bathroom was decorated in mermaids.

Tegan wondered if running water would drown out her puking.

Her breathing filled the room, echoed off the tile. She sat on the edge of the tub and took deep breaths in through her nose, exhaling through her mouth, until her body relaxed

She wondered how long she'd been gone. Did Rileigh know something was up? She reached over and flushed the toilet, then ripped off her clothes. She avoided looking in the mirror.

The swimsuit was looser than Tegan remembered. She stood straighter, filled with pride. *Maybe this is making me lose weight.* She'd keep alternating between starving herself and throwing up until she was comfortable, then she'd stop.

And if she was never comfortable, she'd do it until she died.

Rileigh knocked on the door.

"Are you ready?" She didn't sound concerned, just excited.

Is she really happy to spend time with me?

Tegan opened the door instead of answering.

Rileigh looked her up and down. Tegan didn't have time to feel bad about herself, because Rileigh's face lit her up.

"Oh my gosh. You look so cute." She reached out and straightened one of Tegan's straps. "Where did you get this?"

Tegan looked down at the unremarkable, cherry-dotted black suit. "I don't remember. I've had it for so long."

Rileigh took it in again, and with an authoritative nod said, "It's cute."

Then it's cute.

Tegan couldn't manage to stop herself from covering her stomach as Rileigh led her to the pool. Small seismic waves shook her thighs.

Rileigh came to a sudden stop at the edge of the pool, turned to face Tegan, and saluted.

Tegan looked behind her and saw Rileigh flop backward into the pool in the reflection of the glass door.

Water sloshed against her feet and shins. The water was cold against her skin, but the sun chased away the sensation before Tegan could even pull away. She edged her way to the stairs.

Rileigh emerged; her hair was laid out like a jellyfish encircling her.

"You don't want to jump in?"

Tegan's foot was already on the first rung. "Oh. No." She shivered as her feet dipped into the frigid water.

"You'll get over the cold quicker that way."

Tegan slid herself into the water. Her teeth chattered, and she felt her nipples stabbing at the fabric of her suit. She submerged herself and came up with crossed arms. But Rileigh was still looking at her as though she was expecting an answer to something.

"I wouldn't want to splash water everywhere."

"My parents don't care. I do it all the time."

"You're smaller than me." The words escaped Tegan's lips before she realized it. She bit her lip hard enough to tear it.

"Well, yeah, but you aren't fat or anything."

Tegan wanted to be back below the water. Wanted to fill her lungs with water. But maybe Rileigh would think her face was red from sunburn and not embarrassment.

But Rileigh wasn't paying attention to her, because she wasn't talking to make Tegan feel better, she was stating it as fact.

She lay on her back and paddled herself to the other end of the pool, the water rippling around her, catching the sunlight like glitter.

Tegan lowered herself beneath the surface and opened her eyes. The chlorine stung, but the sight of Rileigh's hair dancing under her body was worth it. The strands reached for her like tentacles, and she longed to run her fingers through it. It wanted her to.

She stayed down on the pool floor until her lungs and eyes burned, until she had no more bubbles to release.

The air couldn't fill her lungs quick enough. She was too greedy, her lungs too deprived, and she coughed until she thought she'd vomit. She clung to the edge of the pool.

Rileigh was floating toward her now, her nose and eyes exposed like a crocodile.

"You ok?" She peaked her mouth above the water. Little droplets landed on Tegan's skin.

"Yeah, just stayed under too long."

"Did you get chlorine up your nose? That's the worst."

"No, just in my eyes."

"You can open your eyes underwater? I'm bad at it. I bet you'd be good with the swim rings."

"Swim rings?"

"You've never played?"

Tegan shook her head.

Rileigh swam to the edge and pulled herself out. She rolled across the hot pavement and disappeared into the shed. She came back clutching four bright yellow rings. She tossed them willy-nilly across the pool. They floated lazily to the bottom.

"I've seen these before."

Rileigh lowered herself over the edge and back into the pool. "Yeah? My dad is really fast at these. Go on." Water sloshed off her arm as she motioned to the deepest part of the deep end.

Tegan lowered herself back under and propelled herself off the wall. She snatched the ring effortlessly and emerged.

Rileigh told her to hang on to it as she dove beneath to grab the one closest to her. It took much longer than Tegan would expect, but she didn't mind. It allowed her to watch Rileigh's hair dance beneath the surface.

And so, it went between the two of them, with bits of conversation sprinkled throughout, until the sun lowered and their skin pruned.

***

Tegan reveled in the warmth her sunburn brought her. She would burn forever if it meant she would be able to spend time with Rileigh.

The two were sprawled out on Rileigh's bedroom floor. The only light came from the multicolored chandelier, which cast odd shadows upon them, like they were bathing beneath stained glass, and the full moon through the bay window.

Rileigh's hair was fanned out beneath her, dry now. It nearly reached Tegan. She could feel it. Just out of her reach. It was reaching for her again.

Rileigh raised herself to her elbows. Tegan did not move, merely followed her with her eyes. She smiled mischievously. "Do you want to play truth or dare?" Her whisper seemed to echo.

Tegan sat up with her. "Sure. I've never done it before."

"It's so much fun. Do you want to go first?"

Tegan's face flushed. The sunburn ached. "No, that's ok. You start."

"Ok, ok. Truth or dare?"

"Um. Truth."

Rileigh sighed dramatically. "Fine."

"No, no. Fine. I'll do dare."

Rileigh's eyes lit up. She looked about her room as if she was being timed. "I dare you to," she grabbed a stuffed rabbit from the foot of her bed and tossed it to Tegan, "practice kissing on Peter."

Tegan squinted into Peter's black button eyes. Rileigh was giggling before Tegan even began. She didn't know what she was doing. She had no interest in kissing. Sometimes she felt flushed when she thought about certain things, but she didn't think they were the right things. She'd never felt that way about anyone, boy or girl. And she didn't think she ever would.

But she wanted to impress, so she just did what she'd seen in cheesy movies, pursing her lips and rubbing her face back and forth on his yarn lined mouth.

Rileigh clapped as she laughed, and Tegan bowed. "Ok, ok, your turn."

Tegan deflated. "Oh, goodness. I don't know."

"Come on. It can be anything."

"I can't think of anything."

"Want me to go again? I'll let you pick truth this time."

"Sure." The overwhelming dread of being made fun of was making her nauseous.

"Truth or dare."

"Truth."

"Do you have a crush on Bailey?"

Tegan recoiled. "God, no."

Rileigh laughed and clapped again. "Come on, he's not that bad."

Tegan shook her head vehemently. "No. I don't like him. I don't like any boys."

"Oh. Do you like girls?"

Tegan was taken aback by the question.

"It's ok if you do," Rileigh assured.

"I don't. I don't like anybody. Not in that way. I've never felt it."

"Really?" Rileigh searched Tegan's face.

"Really." Tegan squirmed under Rileigh's gaze.

"Oh, thank goodness. Me either."

A warmth spread through Tegan like she'd never felt before. Maybe she wasn't as weird as she thought.

"So, you're asexual too?"

Rileigh pulled her golden mane back into a ponytail. "I don't know. I really don't. I just know that I don't think about those things. I don't want them."

"Ever?"

"I think so."

Tegan's face hurt from smiling; the raw skin pulled at itself.

"Why are you smiling so big?"

"I've never known anyone else who felt that way. It makes me ...feel...normal."

"You don't think you're normal?" Rileigh wrapped her arms around her knees.

Tegan cleared her throat. She focused on the white carpet. "Not really, no."

"Why not?"

Tegan shrugged. "I don't know. I just feel outside of things, you know?"

Rileigh nodded her head vigorously. Her ponytail tickled her back. "I totally get what you mean."

Tegan laughed. "No way."

"Yes way. I feel like I don't have any friends." She gave a small smile when her voice caught.

"But everybody likes you."

"Everybody? No. I don't think so. I'm friendly with people is all. No one makes an effort outside of class. I care so much about what people think of me. I think they can sense that, you know? I think it drives them away."

Tegan nodded her head. She bit her bottom lip and wrapped her arms around her torso. "I think you just think about it too much."

"You're probably right. That's why I like you so much."

Tegan cocked her head.

"Because you don't care if people like you or not."

Tegan's laugh was bitter enough to burn her throat.

Rileigh smiled. "And that's why people like you."

"People don't like me, Rileigh. Only you do. I feel like people are staring at me all the time. But then again I don't feel like anyone really sees me."

Rileigh furrowed her brow. "People like you. They think you're brilliant. And you know how brilliant people can be."

Tegan couldn't help but grin and shake her head. They were crazy. All of them. "Sure, sure. Let's get back to the game. Truth or dare?"

"Hmmmm. Truth."

"All right. Is it true that you're going to the dance with Austin in a few weeks?"

Rileigh pretended to gag. "No way. I'm not going to that shit. Definitely not with him."

Tegan gasped at the unexpected curse word and erupted into a fit of giggles.

Rileigh pushed her playfully. "What?"

"You cussing."

"What about it?" Her smile could have lit up the room.

"Just not something I'd expect."

Rileigh shook her head. "You must think I'm really good."

"You aren't?"

"The best of us aren't."

Rileigh had scooted closer to Tegan, and Tegan could feel electricity in the space separating them. She wanted to reach out and touch her, to be comforted by human contact, but she remained rooted.

"So, how come your mom didn't come?"

Thoughts of her mother full of tubes flashed before her eyes. She closed her eyes tightly, hoping that they would disappear in a flash of colorful dots. "She's dead."

Rileigh exhaled. "I'm sorry. I didn't know."

"Most people don't. It's ok."

Rileigh scooted closer to her again. "What happened?"

Tegan opened her eyes. "Cancer."

"Was it long ago?"

"No. We moved here right after. My dad couldn't take being in the same place, you know?"

"What about you?"

Tegan stiffened and stared at the moon, avoiding eye contact. "What about me?"

"Well, are you ok?"

Her body felt tight enough to snap. She remained perfectly still. "I'm ok."

A silence filled the room. It was suffocating, like a summer night when cicada screams would fill the air.

"You know, if you're ever not feeling ok, I'm here for you." Rileigh reached forward and wrapped her arms around Tegan.

She wanted to run from the touch, to scream until everything went black, because she knew that Rileigh would be able to feel the bad inside of Tegan radiating through her skin. But she didn't. And Rileigh didn't let go. Slowly Tegan's body began to unwind, part by part, and she rested her head upon Rileigh's and the two stayed like that for a long time.

"I'm tired." Tegan finally managed.

Rileigh unwrapped herself from Tegan, and they both immediately missed the warmth and the weight.

"Where am I sleeping?"

"With me, silly. Haven't you ever been to a sleepover?"

Tegan looked at the floor. "No."

Rileigh pulled back the covers and slid into bed. She patted the spot beside her. "Come on."

Tegan positioned herself as far away from Rileigh as she could, her body barely clinging to the edge of the bed.

Rileigh shook her head and giggled. "Goodnight."

"Goodnight."

The moon basked Tegan in a heavenly glow. She stared at her pale arms and hands, and for the first time in a long time, admired how beautiful she was. Beautiful parts. She felt Rileigh shift in the bed. Her breathing had slowed and deepened.

Tegan finally felt confident enough to turn her head. She imagined Rileigh would be staring back disapprovingly, judging her for trying to spy, but she wasn't. In fact, she wasn't even facing Tegan anymore. Her ponytail filled the space between them.

Tegan's breath caught. If Rileigh's hair was beautiful in the sunlight, it was supernaturally so in the glow of the moon. Her middle ached looking at it. A perfection she could never reach.

Her daydream of her and Rileigh melting together infiltrated her mind. Unobtainable.

But maybe there was another way to carry Rileigh with her. To be a part of Rileigh.

Carefully, slowly, she slid out of bed. Rileigh's hairbrush sat on her dresser, and in it were countless strands of beautiful, white hair.

Never apart.

Tegan pulled a small clump of the hair out and forced it into her mouth. She did not chew. It went down better than expected. She tightened from the pelvis up.

She sat the brush back and crawled back into bed. This time she allowed herself to relax, and her legs rested gently against Rileigh's.

CHAPTER 6

SUMMER BREAK STARTS AT three o'clock today. And it will start the countdown to my suicide.

Tegan had grown closer to Rileigh in the six weeks since their first slumber party. Rileigh had changed her in ways she never knew possible. Tegan had thinned out and learned to walk with a straight back and a high head. She'd begun to straighten her hair and cared for it regularly. Rileigh had taught her how to put mascara on, and when Tegan passed her reflection, she didn't turn away in disgust.

But she'd done more than changed her appearance. She'd changed the way people saw her and how they communicated with her. She'd also changed how Tegan felt about people. She wasn't afraid of making eye contact anymore. And she could manage to hold conversations with people other than her father or Rileigh.

But that would all end soon. Summer began in only a few hours and she would go back to being invisible. It would be like every summer before after the move, where she'd lock herself in her room, read books, and sleep her depression away.

It was hard enough to believe people wanted to talk to her at school (and boy did they, after she and Rileigh became close), and it was impossible to think they wouldn't forget about her as soon as she was out of sight.

And if she sank as low as she did the previous summer, she would just kill herself. The thought of leaving her dad made her throat close, but she was probably just a burden on him anyway.

Warm hands encircled her, and a cascade of beautiful gold hair fell around her.

"Hey, Teg." Rileigh's lips touched the side of Tegan's head.

Tegan clasped Rileigh's hands in hers. "Hey."

Rileigh pulled away and dropped in the seat beside her. "What's wrong?"

"What? Nothing. Just zoning out."

Their teachers had already checked out for the year. They watched the clock more closely than any of the students, who had split off in groups to record dumb videos on their phones or cruise the internet.

"I can't wait until summer."

"Yeah."

"So, you're definitely coming to my birthday party, right?" Rileigh leaned forward, cradling her head in her hands. Her big, blue eyes blinked and searched Tegan's face.

"Oh. Yeah. In two weeks, right?"

"Right. I'm excited. My parents are letting me have a slumber party this year, too, which you have to come to, of course."

"Of course." Tegan's ears burned. Rileigh seemed to stare into her soul.

Rileigh's perfectly plump lips parted to reveal very straight, very white teeth. "What's up with you today, dude?"

Tegan let her hair fall in her face to shield her. "I don't know. Just used to everyone forgetting about me in the summer." She didn't know how Rileigh did that—made her confess things.

"Oh, Teg." Rileigh leaned forward and wrapped her arms tightly around Tegan. "You silly thing. I'd never forget you. Besides, summer would suck without you. There's no one else I'd rather be lazy with."

Tegan's body relaxed as Rileigh's hair spilled over their shoulders and tickled Tegan's back. "You know how I get."

The bell finally released the teachers and other students from their torment. People nearly knocked their desks over as they rushed to the door.

Rileigh had detached herself from Tegan and was already standing before Tegan had had a chance to pack up her supplies.

"Wanna come over tomorrow?" Rileigh pulled her hair back into a loose ponytail that laid flat against her neck.

Tegan straightened her outfit, which was nearly identical to Rileigh's, just in a different color. "Yeah, totally."

Rileigh beamed. "This is gonna be the best summer ever."

***

The best summer ever.

Tegan admired herself in the full-length mirror in her bathroom. The new bikini fit her like a second skin. The yellow made her newly tanned skin glow. She'd never been tan before. She hadn't really been much of an outside kid until Rileigh.

Rileigh was constantly dragging her out to the pool or having her hike around the surrounding woods and fields with her. Not that Tegan minded. No. Being kissed by the warm rays of the sun was about as close as she could get to being held in the golden bliss of Rileigh's hair.

She'd straightened her hair, which had finally made it past her shoulders, but she wasn't sure why. As soon as she got it wet, it would immediately reset to her terrible natural waves. But that was the way the kids at school knew her now. An olive-skinned, dark-haired clone of Rileigh. That was as close as she could get.

Her dad knocked on the door.

"You about ready, kid?"

"Yeah. Was just trying on my new suit."

"Again?"

"Shut up, Dad."

He chuckled, and Tegan listened as he stomped back downstairs.

She turned her attention back to the mirror and ran her hand over her smooth stomach. She never thought she'd be able to look in the mirror and not be driven to vomit. She still forced herself to throw up about once a week, just to keep her body in check, but the upswing in physical activity, and the very minimal amount of food she consumed, had really thinned her out.

She pulled a pair of cut off jean shorts and a tank top on over the suit.

The phone downstairs rang. She hadn't yet been able to convince her dad to get her a cellphone. She'd barely managed to convince him to get himself one.

"Teg! Phone for you!" Her dad hollered up the stairs.

Tegan sprinted to her room. "I'm about to pick up!" She flopped onto her bed. "Hello?"

"Where are you?"

Tegan heard the *click* as her dad hung up the downstairs phone. "I'm about to leave."

"You're gonna be late."

"Barely." Her stomach was in knots thinking about all the people that would be at Rileigh's.

"I wanted you to be here early to help me greet people."

"But it isn't my house."

"No, but I'd feel better if you were here with me when everyone starts to come. I get anxious, you know."

Tegan wanted to laugh, but held it back by pinching her stomach. "I'll leave as soon as I hang up."

"Promise? You aren't ditching me?"

"Me? Ditch you? Come on, now."

Rileigh's light tinkling laugh filled the quiet of Tegan's room. Tegan couldn't help but smile.

"Ok. I'll hang up then."

But she didn't. Tegan had to hang up. It was always that way. She didn't say goodbye.

Her dad was already in the truck waiting. "Finally decide to join me?"

"Har har." She tossed her bag in the space between them and cranked the window down.

"Did you take your medicine today?"

Tegan acted like she didn't hear him.

He reached across and grabbed her leg. "Hey."

"No."

"You're awful nervous today. You need to take it. It'll make you feel better."

"I'm getting better, Dad."

"I know you are. But if you don't keep up with it, you could backslide. I wouldn't want that to happen. We all have bad days, you know?"

Tegan tore through her bag. The bottle was wrapped up in a pair of socks at the bottom. Rileigh knew that she took medication, but nobody else at school did. The last thing she wanted was for all the girls at the slumber party to find out. They'd think she was crazy. They'd know Rileigh pitied her and that's why they were so close.

She felt guilty as soon as the thought crossed her mind. Rileigh wasn't like that. Tegan's brain was just being unruly again. Her dad was right.

She tossed a pill back and rehid the bottle.

Her dad reached across and squeezed her shoulder. "Thank you."

"You're not gonna dip out on your therapy session because I won't be home, will you?"

"That was once. I go while you're at school, usually. I'm not the one who has to be reminded to take care of themselves." He pinched her playfully.

"Sometimes you do."

He sighed. "You're a good kid. But you don't need to be worrying about me."

"I always will. Someone's gotta keep you in check. Otherwise, who'd feed me?"

Her dad snorted. "Shut up."

Tegan leaned her head out the open window, soaking in the sun, smiling through the breeze.

Cars were pulling in and out of Rileigh's driveway in near perfect rotation. The bottom of Tegan's stomach cramped. Her hand instinctively covered it. But she quickly removed it before her dad could bring up how she should have taken her medicine sooner.

She took in a deep breath, held it, and exhaled until her vision started to blur. The buzzing in her ears stifled.

She flung the door open with such force that the truck rocked noticeably. She looked back at her dad sheepishly.

He could have chastised her then; could have tried to smother her with a heart to heart in front of her classmates that were rushing to the house. But he didn't. The idea came to him, clouded his eyes, but he let it go, and simply said, "Have fun, kid. I'm just a phone call away if it gets too hard. I can always say I need your help with something real quick so you have a few minutes to breathe. I'll make it inconspicuous."

A lump rose in Tegan's throat, and she was overcome by the urge to throw her arms around him and cry while he cradled her to sleep like he'd done after her mother had died. But instead she swallowed the lump, grabbed her bag, and mouthed "thank you."

He started to tell her that he loved her, but he mouthed it instead. She looked around to make sure that there was no one paying attention to her and blew him a quick kiss.

"Tegan! Rileigh will be so happy that you've made it." Rileigh's mom greeted her at the door. "Shoes off, please." She pointed at a kid who was trying to walk through the dining room. She smiled at Tegan, but it was strained. Just lips pulled back over teeth. Her eyes roamed, trying to keep track of the chaos of all the people shuffling through her house.

Tegan kicked her shoes off and looked back into the living room. "Where is Rileigh?"

"Oh, she's in the pool already."

Tegan followed her into the kitchen. There were opened bags of snacks scattered all over the counter. She began to fill a jug with water as she opened a few cabinets looking for lemonade, which was situated at the front of the first cabinet she'd opened.

"Can I help you with something?"

"What?" The jug had overfilled. She slammed the faucet down and pulled her hair out of her face.

"What can I help with?"

"Oh, nothing, honey. You go out and have fun with everybody." She whipped back around at the sound of the front door opening again.

"Hey, I can make the lemonade if you need to go direct people. Were you going to refill the snack bowls too? Should I do that?"

"Tegan, you don't have to—shoes off, please!" She rushed to the door as more kids filtered in.

Tegan dumped half the water out of the jug and made the lemonade. She could hear Rileigh's mom talking to another parent, explaining how late the boys would be able to stay, and harping on everyone to please remove their shoes.

Tegan carried the jug out to the deck, which was soaked from what she was sure were countless cannonballs.

And there was Rileigh, in the center of the pool, surrounded by people. Her skin glistened in the sun, which was barely a match for her dazzling smile. Her hair was pulled back in a high ponytail so that only the tip dipped beneath the surface of the water.

Their eyes met. Somehow her smile brightened. Her eyes sparkled. "Tegan!" She waved at her, splashing a girl in their history class, Meghan, on accident. She swam through the ten or so kids that were already in the water to the edge of the pool. She grinned up at Tegan. "You finally showed."

"I told you I would."

"What are you doing? Get in."

"I'm gonna help your mom for a sec. She seems kind of stressed out."

"Oh, Teg. You're a real-life angel."

The way Rileigh looked up her made her stomach flip like she'd just dropped on a rollercoaster. She swayed under the rush of adrenaline. *How can someone so perfect look at me like that? What must that be like? To have perfect skin, perfect hair, a perfect smile? To know that people like you because you are a warm pool or perfection and not because someone tells you that you must?*

"Hey, Tegan." Bailey was standing a few feet away from her.

She pulled back. "Hi."

He filled the space she had created between them. "Are you gonna swim?" His trunks were bright blue with tiny yellow pineapples dotted throughout. His chest was pale and sparsely freckled.

Looking at his body make Tegan feel cold. "I'm just helping Rileigh's mom with some stuff."

"Oh, sweet, you need any help?" He reached for an empty chip bowl.

But Tegan snatched it up before his fingers could touch it. "No. I'm good thanks."

For a moment he looked as though he were about to hit her. His eyes filled with a fire and hatred Tegan had only seen in herself, and she could see the muscles in his jaw tense. But just as quickly as the darkness overtook him, it was gone.

"See you in the pool then." He took a running start toward it.

Droplets of water slammed into the glass door as Tegan crossed inside.

She filled the three bowls with snacks and cradled them as best she could to go back out.

Rileigh's mom rushed back into the kitchen. Her blonde hair, a lighter shade than Rileigh's, and definitely dyed, was sticking up at odd angles. She ran her fingers through it and reached for the cabinet Tegan had retrieved the snacks from. She was so wrapped up in the chaos that she hadn't even noticed that Tegan was in the room.

"Mrs. Kinane?"

Rileigh's mom jumped and spun around. She grabbed a bowl from Tegan's hand. "Oh, honey, you didn't have to do this."

"It's ok. I don't mind helping."

She smiled at Tegan. Her smile wasn't breathtaking like Rileigh's, she got that from her dad, but it created a single dimple and was beautiful in its own way.

The two were nearly splashed as they made their way to the snack table.

"You think we should close the door?" She looked at the line waiting to jump off the diving board.

Tegan shrugged. "People are probably gonna be going in and out to use the bathroom anyway."

She sighed. "You're right. The house is going to get soaked no matter what." The two watched the guests scream and splash. "You know, Tegan, you're a good girl."

Tegan cleared her throat. "Oh. Thank you."

Mrs. Kinane gripped her shoulder. "We're so happy that you are Rileigh found each other."

Tegan felt as though she was burning under Mrs. Kinane's loving gaze. She thought of her mother, with her sunken eyes and yellow skin looking at her the same way. Her vision blacked out and she swayed a little. She needed to throw up.

"Mom! Leave Tegan alone." Rileigh was propped up on the edge of the pool again,

Her mother released Tegan. "I'm sorry to keep you, dear. Thank you so much for helping out. You must be dying to get in the pool."

The vomit still sat at the bottom of Tegan's throat. "It's ok." She pulled her shirt off and shimmied out of her jean shorts before another conversation started.

"Ooooo. Look at Tegan." Rileigh catcalled from the pool. She splashed at her. "You can't come to my birthday party and be cuter than me!"

People were joining in on the fun, looking Tegan up and down and whistling.

"Looking good." Bailey leered at her.

Tegan wondered what it would be like to peel herself out of her skin. To feel the layers separate, and to hear the wet noise it would make as it shed.

Her fingers itched to tug at her stomach. But, conscious of all the eyes on her, she simply lowered herself down beside Rileigh and slid into the pool.

The water was cold, and it shocked her system at first. She lowered herself beneath the surface, wanting to feel the tingling sensation of her skin tightening, wanting to linger on the slight pain that it caused.

When she came back up Rileigh was right beside her, smiling. She flung her arms around her and nearly pulled her back under. "Come on. Let's jump off the diving board together."

And just like that Tegan was the center of Rileigh's universe again, just as Rileigh was to Tegan. The other people there did not matter. They were fillers. Set dressing. Rileigh and Tegan. That was all that mattered.

***

The last boy finally left as the sun dipped beneath the horizon. Tegan watched the car pull away from the bathroom window. Rileigh's parents had hosed the girls down as Rileigh had taken a shower.

They'd insisted that Tegan take a shower as well. Her dad had probably told them about how she could get if she didn't feel clean. How she'd pick at her skin.

But she wasn't embarrassed. She didn't care if the adults knew. To her knowledge every adult who came into contact with her knew about her medication. They had to keep an eye on her.

Amanda Batcho had monopolized Rileigh's time since she'd exited the shower. She'd shoved her way in between the two of them when they crowded around the table to eat ice cream. Tegan had waited until hers turned to a chocolate soup to even begin prodding at it. She'd washed most of it down the sink. No one noticed.

She sat on the toilet seat and cradled her head in her hands. She wanted Rileigh's attention, but she didn't know how to get it back. She couldn't bear to be dramatic or to express her feelings about the situation. She'd suffer in silence.

She pulled back the mermaid shower curtain and stiffened. A perfect ball of Rileigh's hair was still bundled up in the drain. Everything was silent; hyper focused.

She plucked the hairball out and rolled it between her fingers. She hoped some of the shine would stick. She hoped it would sink into her fingers and color her whole body; make her brighter.

But her skin remained the same olive color it had been.

But you've already changed so much since you started this. This could be it. This could make you her. No. Make you one.

She checked to make sure the door was locked and sat the ball on her tongue. She turned the water on. Steam rose from the tub floor.

Tegan rolled the ball around in her mouth as she stripped. She stood there for a while, being naked and pure with the ball pressed between her tongue and the roof of her mouth. Her nipples hardened.

She swallowed the ball as she stepped into the shower.

The water embraced and hid her.

***

The house was dark and quiet. Tegan had had to sit and listen to the girls flirt with Rileigh's dad. They had giggled too loudly at his jokes and tried to include him in conversations. Tegan respected the idea of wanting to spend time with an older man for conversation. But she didn't know why anyone would want to be with a man in any other way, no matter the age.

The lack of sexual attraction was isolating. She couldn't connect on what seemed to be the most common level of the people around her. She loved the idea of people, and loved certain things about them, but the idea of someone touching her made her want to shrink into herself until she disappeared.

Usually, she had Rileigh. She felt the same. And Tegan thought that it was a perfect time for them to come back together because, obviously, neither of them was attracted to her dad. But Amanda still occupied her time, barely allowing anyone else to get a word in with her. When the girls huddled together on the living room floor to watch a scary movie, Amanda had forced Rileigh into the corner seat of the couch (Rileigh would never sit there on her own, she liked the middle seat, and Tegan knew that) and plopped down beside her, essentially cutting her off from Tegan.

Adhira Zina had tried her best to keep Tegan company throughout the evening, though. Tegan didn't mind Adhira. She was shy too, and incredibly smart in math and science, the things Tegan was decent at, but not great. Tegan loved sitting beside her, seeing how Adhira's dark skin looked next to her's. She loved the perfect, black hair that rested in the middle of her back in a loose braid. If she thought that she could ever be close to Adhira, her obsession might have been with her and not Rileigh. Maybe she'd have someone who could both understand and see the flip side of her life, of her thoughts.

But that wasn't how things worked out. And now they were all asleep. Except Tegan, who lay on her side and stared through the kitchen, to the sliver of the sliding glass door.

She imagined someone coming in and slitting their throats as they slept. How the man would be quiet enough to not wake them. How he would see their eyes wide with fear in their last moments, like a horse off to the slaughter. How he would see her eyes staring up at him before the knife touched her skin, and the sickly smile that would spread across his face, how his eyes would be wild, electric even.

"Teg."

The whisper was so soft that Tegan was sure it had to be a ghost. She lay perfectly still, waiting to hear it again so she could decide whether to ignore or it or get up and call her dad to come pick her up.

"Teg." It was louder this time. And the voice was finally recognizable.

She pushed herself up onto her elbows. Rileigh was sitting on the staircase, her face pressed between the bottom two bars. She motioned for Tegan to come closer.

Still not sure whether or not some ghost was trying to lure her into a premature death, but unwilling to spurn Rileigh, she tiptoed across the wood floor.

"What are you doing?"

She held her hand through the bars. "Will you come to my room with me?"

Tegan didn't answer, she simply followed Rileigh up the stairs and down the hall.

Rileigh closed the door slowly as to not make any noise. She slid into her bed. Tegan followed.

"Thanks for coming. I didn't want to sleep alone. I keep thinking about that movie."

A bitter vile burned in Tegan's throat. "You didn't want Amanda to come up?"

Rileigh snorted a little louder than she intended. "Oh, my god. She'd been so annoying tonight."

"Yeah?"

"Yeah. You saw how she followed me around all night, right? I can't believe you didn't save me." She punched Tegan in the arm playfully.

Tegan grinned and wormed beneath the sheets. "I thought you enjoyed it."

"Asshole." Rileigh lay down beside her, smiling at her. Their faces were so close. Tegan felt as though a force, something electric, was pulling them together. She imagined her jaw unhinging, swallowing Rileigh whole.

Rileigh's smile remained, but it shifted. It no longer touched her eyes. No, there was something mean (or hurt?) in them now. "I saw you cozied up with Adhira."

Tegan grinned. "I like Adhira, yes."

Rileigh huffed.

"What?"

"You didn't save me so that you could have fun with her." She didn't totally believe what she was saying. But she didn't completely disbelieve it either. When she'd told Tegan months before she didn't feel important to anyone, months before she had meant it. She was a fixture in people's lives, sure, but not for long, and certainly not in a deep way like she had with Tegan. She didn't want to lose that.

"You're crazy." As if possessed by something, Tegan reached out to brush a strand of Rileigh's hair behind her ear. Her skin burned at the contact. It made her stomach and thighs tighten. She wanted her pores to open and Rileigh's hair to burrow deep beneath her skin.

Rileigh giggled and snuggled up against Tegan. Tegan didn't know how to respond, so she didn't.

The silence between them was so long that Tegan was sure that Rileigh had fallen asleep.

But, without moving her head from Tegan's throat, Rileigh said, "I better be your favorite."

"Always." Tegan wrapped an arm around Rileigh now, hoping that she could manage to sink into her.

CHAPTER 7

"WHAT DO YOU THINK of Jeff Hinmon?" Rileigh was admiring herself in the mirror. She wore a pair of shorts and a shirt that cut off near the bottom of her ribs. She ran her fingers down her tight stomach.

Tegan didn't think anything of him, but she knew why Rileigh was asking her. "What do you think of him?"

Rileigh turned around with a smile that warmed the room. She dropped down on her knees in front of Tegan, who was sitting on the edge of Rileigh's bed, painting her fingernails. "Oh, Teg, I like him a lot."

"I thought you didn't like boys." She smeared a line of black polish on the edge of her finger.

"I grew out of that."

Tegan had to bite the inside of her mouth to keep a sob from escaping her. The way she had said it was so pointed. *I grew out of that...haven't you?* Well, no, she hadn't. She still didn't feel anything, for anyone. And she never thought she would.

I thought we were the same.

"Oh." She felt like she had to say something. Rileigh was staring into her. Tegan wondered what she saw in there. Was it rotten, purple and yellow, like her mother's skin had been before she passed? Or was it just warm liquid, running on an endless loop, coating her organs.

She felt a tension between her legs and pulled them shut tighter. The tension increased.

"Don't you like anyone yet?"

"No. I told you I wouldn't."

"But things change sometimes, don't they?"

"Not that."

Rileigh bit her bottom lip and rested her hands on Tegan's knees. The black polish bottle was saved by her thigh. She looked up at

Tegan as though in prayer. Her rainbow chandelier caught the sunlight and cast a glow across her face.

"I need to tell you something."

Everything in Tegan tensed. Her knees pressed together hard, lifting Rileigh's hands up with them. *This is it. She's finally going to realize that I'm not worth her time. She's going to push me away. Her dad will take me home, and I'll run a warmth bath, slide in, and slit my wrists.*

She made a low noise in her throat that vibrated throughout her chest. She couldn't open her mouth without it trembling.

"I'm going on a date with Jeff tonight."

The buildup to her heartbreak was too slow. Her skin felt tight. "That's fine. My dad can pick me up whenever." It was barely more than a whisper.

"Promise you won't be mad at me."

Tegan squeezed her eyes hard enough to make bursts of color explode in the darkness.

"Teg?"

Rileigh carefully removed the black bottle from Tegan's lap and screwed the top back on. Tegan hadn't realized that her fists were clenched until Rileigh tenderly pulled her fingers out of her palms and forced their hands together.

Tegan was concentrating on breathing out of her nose without sounding like she was hyperventilating. Her lips were pressed together tightly, so tightly that they were grinding against her teeth. "Hmm?" she managed.

"You remember Bailey? He was in our science class? And my birthday party?"

Tegan's eyes flew open. Her teeth grinded together involuntarily. Loud enough for Rileigh to hear. *What is this?*

"Well, he really likes you. And he's the only boy I've ever seen you even talk around. And he's Jeff cousin."

It took a minute for Tegan to understand her. Rileigh had spoken so fast that it all seemed to come out as one big word. "Bailey?"

"Well, I kind of thought we could go on a double date."

Tegan's hands went limp in Rileigh's. "You want me to go on a date with him?"

Rileigh squeezed Tegan's hands and scooted forward. Her elbows dug into Tegan's knees. "Please, Teg, please? My parents won't let me hang out with Jeff alone and Bailey likes you so much. You like him too. I can tell."

Tegan ripped her hands out of their embrace. "I do *not like* him." Spittle flew from her mouth and onto Rileigh's face.

If she felt it, she did not react. "Please do this for me. If you don't like him, you never have to do it again, ok? I promise."

Tegan tried to swallow but her mouth was too dry. She coughed violently. She rushed to the bathroom as she began to gag. She stuck her face beneath the faucet and let the cold water battle down the bile.

Rileigh was beside her with a towel. She didn't speak as Tegan cleaned her face. She waited until Tegan had meticulously folded it before asking, "Are you all right?"

"I think so. Just choked."

Rileigh stood rooted where she was as Tegan went back to the room and sat on the edge of the bed where she'd been. She watched as Tegan finished painting her fingernails, as if nothing had happened.

But a wave of relief had washed over Tegan when the bile was washed down. This wasn't the worst-case scenario. Rileigh still wanted her around. She wanted her around so badly, in fact, that she was willing to share her time with her romantic interest with Tegan. The idea of Bailey touching her or kissing her made her want to pick at her skin, but she could at least pretend to like him if it meant that her time with Rileigh didn't have to be over.

She hadn't gotten enough of her yet. There was still so much to absorb.

Rileigh sat down on the bed beside her. Her lower lip quivered. "I'm sorry. I can tell them not to come if you want."

Tegan heard the hitch in her voice and reached over to rub her back. "It's ok, Rileigh. I'm sorry I scared you. You don't have to cancel your date. I'll do it."

"You will?" The tears that had been sitting on the edge of her eyes, threatening to spill over with every passing second, nearly immediately disappeared. "You don't have to if you really don't want to. You know that, right?" She wiped at her eyes.

"Yes. I want to. I think it would be fun to go on a double date."

Rileigh threw her arms around Tegan and buried her face in her stomach. "Thank you so much. You're the best friend ever."

Tegan shivered with delight at the compliment.

***

An hour later Rileigh had just finished putting the finishing touches on Tegan's makeup. "Go look," she beamed.

Tegan walked to the full-length mirror but did not look at her face. She did not want to trick herself into thinking that her normal face was unworthy like so many others did after they saw their face with makeup on.

"It's wonderful." She'd already turned away from her reflection.

As if by magic or fate the girls heard a knock downstairs at the front door.

Rileigh gripped Tegan's forearms. "They're here."

The way her eyes sparkled brightly beneath the dark mascara was enough to chase the knot in Tegan's stomach away.

"Girls!" Rileigh's mother called up the stairs.

The boys waited at the foot of the stairs like good boys do.

Tegan felt Bailey's gaze climb up and down her body. She wanted to cover up, to shrink away, but to do so would be an admittance of weakness. There was something sick in boys that wanted girls more when they did not want to be wanted.

Rileigh was beaming up at Jeff from the landing before Tegan had made it halfway down.

You're doing this for her. Just remember that. Remember how it felt to be alone. Remember how it felt before she was part of you. The knot in her stomach was tighter than usual.

"You kids getting in the pool?" Rileigh's mom asked. Her eyes darted back to the kitchen. Her mind was already rushing through all the things she'd have to prepare to make sure she was seen as a good hostess.

"I think we're just going to go for a walk, mom. Maybe I can show them the pond and the old barn in the back of the property." Rileigh spoke much too fast.

Her mother looked to Tegan. Her warm blue eyes searched Tegan's but found no hint of a lie. *Keep her safe,* they said.

Her gaze hit the floor as she shuffled out behind the others. She didn't care what Rileigh did with her body, as long as she could have her time. And her hair.

Bailey tried to snake his arm around her torso when they were off the deck and what he seemed to think was far enough away from the house. Tegan pulled away as though burned and went to the other side of Rileigh.

Rileigh slipped her hand into Tegan's and gave it a squeeze. Her palms were sweaty, and her fingernails dug into Tegan's palm. Tegan squeezed back.

It made her feel better to know that she made Rileigh feel safe. But if she was this nervous around a boy that she liked, how did women stand to be around men at all?

Jeff tried to make small talk to alleviate the silence, but Tegan didn't listen. The humidity was suffocating her, and she realized that she had to breathe through her mouth to get the proper amount of air. Sweat had already formed above her top lip and on her forehead. She wondered how long it would take before she would sweat off the ridiculous makeup.

Once they'd nearly reached the pond, Rileigh released Tegan's hand and took Jeff's instead. Tegan made no move to get closer to Bailey. She wished he hadn't come. She hated the way his eyes lingered on her. It made her feel dirty for some reason. Like she'd done something wrong. Angry bile climbed up her throat. Why should she have to feel bad for a boy not being able to control his gaze? What was it inside her that made her wilt beneath it? *Because he will look and imagine even if you don't want him to. There's no way to stop it. And if you tried, he could hurt you.*

That much was true. Bailey had played baseball over the summer and had become somewhat of a star player. He'd picked up some weights and was looking into the track team for when school started back up. He looked a bit older than the others, especially Jeff who was thin and waifish, in a way that made adults refer to him as "a handsome young man."

He slowed his pace so that he could slide behind Jeff and Rileigh and closer to Tegan. She tried to slow her pace as well, so that there would be three tiny lines of teenagers, but he simply matched her steps.

He walked so close beside her that their arms touched slightly with each step. The contact made Tegan nauseous. She pressed a hand on her stomach, over the ball of hair, the pieces of Rileigh that stayed with her. Maybe it would have calmed her if he wouldn't have intertwined their fingers.

Tegan looked to Rileigh to save her, but Rileigh was clinging to Jeff. Their faces were close, and they smiled through their whispers.

"Why'd you put on makeup?" Bailey's voice broke the white noise of the bugs around them.

"I didn't."

Bailey slowed his pace even further so that he could examine her face. Tegan's eyes tried to look anywhere but his face. Everything inside her hardened, making it difficult for her to breathe. Rileigh and

Jeff were getting farther and farther away. Soon they would be at the little dock that sat along the pond and Bailey and Tegan would be lost to the wilderness. Disappeared. Swallowed by the knot inside her.

"I like your natural face better."

I didn't ask. "Rileigh put it on."

He pulled her closer. She wondered how people could like being this close to one another. She didn't feel as though she could walk properly with his hip pressing against hers.

Rileigh patted the dock beside her, and Tegan dropped in relief. But she wasn't able to relax any of her tight muscles as Bailey pressed himself beside her. He rested his hand on her thigh. Tegan shoved it off, so he pressed it against her knee.

Tegan fought the urge to scream. She squeezed her eyes shut and could see herself, exhaling all the hair inside her, grabbing Bailey, and holding him beneath the surface. The hair would slide back into her like a snake, hiding her power.

Rileigh squeezed Tegan's other knee and brought her back. Jeff's arm was wrapped around Rileigh, his fingers grazing Tegan's side. She hated this sensation of being touched by everyone. It was suffocating. She wished that she could fold in on herself, or maybe even pull all her limbs in like a turtle. Would they run?

Rileigh leaned her head against Tegan's shoulder. A waterfall of gold splashed down Tegan's chest and her nipples hardened. She rested her head against Rileigh's.

The air was thick and moist, but every so often a breeze would come from the back of the property and cool the sweat on their skin. The world around them smelled of wet ground and peonies. And Tegan could smell the sweet vanilla sugar body spray that Rileigh had spritzed all over the both of them. It was mixed with sparkles, so the moonlight hit their collar bones and made them seem magical.

In one swift motion Rileigh lifted away from Tegan and Bailey pulled her closer to him. He smelled like a generic teenage boy, a mix of sweat and too much body spray, and Tegan had to suppress the urge to take a chunk out of his chest.

Rileigh and Jeff towered above Tegan and Bailey.

Rileigh might have felt bad for Tegan if she wasn't so giddy about how low Jeff's hand had traveled down the small of her back.

"Where are you going?" Tegan spoke much louder than she had meant to.

"We're just gonna go for a walk and talk a bit. We'll be back in a few." Rileigh tried to ignore the way Tegan looked at her. *This must be the way that dogs look up at their owners when they drop them off at the pound.*

Tegan tried to listen to their footsteps, to see how far they would go, but the noise was muffled by Bailey's heart pounding against her ear.

She pulled away from his chest but the arm around her waist held her tight to him.

"Where are you going?"

"It's too hot to be pressed against you."

He released his grip on her a little. Their legs were barely touching now. The silence Tegan wanted to drown out Bailey was washed out by the sound of crickets and small animals rustling through the grass.

"I always knew you liked me, you know."

Tegan turned slowly, stiffly, as if only her head was on a swivel. She stared at him with wide eyes, caught between wanting to laugh or spit in his face. "How is that?" The breeze blew a few strands of hair across her face.

"I feel like I'm one of the only people you talked to last year. Before you and Rileigh got close."

The shock had worn off enough for the laughing to win over the spitting. It was sharp and harsh, a noise like a knife cutting through the darkness. "You were the one who talked to me."

"Well, you talked back." She could tell she had hurt his feelings. His voice was small and bitter.

"I was just being polite. I don't like you. I'm doing this because Rileigh asked me to. She was worried that her parents wouldn't let her hang out with Jeff alone."

Even the bugs were quiet now. Bailey let his hand unfurl from Tegan's waist. She used this opportunity to scoot further away from him.

"Doing this for Rileigh." He echoed her words.

But expelling her hatred from him had freed Tegan and she barely noticed. She was transfixed on the reflection of the moon in the pond. For the first time in a week or more she felt like she could really breathe, like her diaphragm was finally able to fully expand. She was almost light-headed, and she swayed in the moonlight to music only she could hear.

Bailey watched the sparkles on her chest and neck catch the moonlight. He wanted to wipe that stupid makeup off her face. "So the rumors are true, huh?"

Tegan stopped swaying and cast a look at Bailey. Her hair swung against her back. "Rumors?" is what came out of her mouth, but really she was thinking, "People think about me? I exist in the minds of others?"

Bailey's smile was sick. Tegan didn't know if it was the lighting that made him look like a ghoul or if she was just seeing a portion of his soul slip through. "That you and Rileigh are together."

Tegan sat up straight. "Together?" There were really people who thought that Tegan was anywhere near worthy to be with Rileigh in such a way?

He leaned closer to her. "Yeah. Together. As in you guys scissor every weekend."

Tegan gasped. "That's heinous."

"Is it? I see the way you look at her."

Tegan hoped that he couldn't see how her face burned in the darkness. "I don't know what you're talking about."

"Then why aren't you looking at me?"

Tegan snapped her gaze up to his in response. But he knew he'd struck a nerve with her. There was something evil within him that knew just the way to twist that to get what he wanted.

"So, you do like her."

"No. I don't like anyone like that. I'm not like that."

"Cut the shit."

His hands were suddenly digging into her arms, so fast she couldn't even remember how they'd gotten there. Or when. But now they were burrowing into her flesh, hooking her to him.

"You're hurting me." She tried to rip herself out of his grip, but her body didn't even move. He was so much bigger than her.

He pressed his lips against her roughly, teeth against teeth. Tegan tried to pull her head back, but she couldn't escape Bailey's grip. Her arms were too far away from him to push off him, so instead she dug her fingernails into his forearms, and hoped that she was digging hard enough to draw blood.

It must have done something because Bailey released his grip on her. As soon as she felt the pressure on how arms disappear, she began to raise herself up. She thought that she'd won.

But Bailey was up too, and he had his arms wrapped tightly around his waist, lifting her feet off the ground.

Tegan opened her mouth to scream, but Bailey must have sensed it because one of his hands slammed over her mouth. Her front tooth sliced open her lip and blood trickled down her throat.

She tried to squirm out of his grasp, but he simply dropped to the ground with her still in his arms. Now his legs pinned her too.

"Now listen here. You like me, don't you?"

Tegan tried to dig an elbow into his ribs. He shook her, hard enough for her to feel something pull in her neck. She stopped straining.

"Good girl. You like me, right. You like me so much you're going to date me. That's the only way you're going to get to see Rileigh anymore, you know? You think she's going to just hang out with you when she can hang out with her boyfriend instead?"

Tegan's body sunk against his. *Not important* flashed through her mind like a neon sign.

"See? You know I'm right." He tugged her until she was seated in his lap. He unwound his legs to free her. "But you know what she would love? To go on double dates. Which means you need a date, and that's me." He stroked her hair with a hand. Tegan was free, but she didn't have the will to run. "And if you don't, I'll tell the entire school that you're gay for her. You think she'd still hang out with you as much if she knew that you thought about getting her naked every time you see her?"

Tegan felt sweat drip down her back. Bile rose in her throat. *Maybe he'll let me go if I puke on him. But, then, what does it matter?* He was right. She was replaceable. And maybe Rileigh wouldn't care if Tegan was gay, but wouldn't she care if she thought Tegan only wanted to be with her to try to get with her?

"Fine," she croaked through his hand.

He released her completely. "What was that?"

"Fine. I'll do it."

His boner pressed into the back of her thighs. "Good. Now kiss me."

She leaned her head back and pressed her mouth, stretched into a tight line, against his.

"We'll work on that." He rubbed where he'd grabbed her earlier. Bruises were already starting to appear.

She didn't know how long she sat there, feeling him pressing into her, thinking about how turned on by twisting her to his will he was, before Rileigh and Jeff emerged silently onto the dock.

"Aww. Look at you two." Rileigh broke the silence. She dropped Jeff's hand and reached out to help Tegan out of Bailey's lap. Tegan let herself be pulled without offering much help.

"You two have fun?" Bailey winked at Jeff.

Jeff grinned and shook his head.

"We better get back to the house or mom will flip. I'm sure your parents will be there by the time we make it back." Rileigh looped an arm through Tegan's and pulled her along. She allowed herself to be led.

"Is it that late already?" Bailey's voice made Tegan want to collapse and shrink herself until she was the nothing she felt she was.

"Did you have fun?" Rileigh whispered into Tegan's ear. But she didn't actually care, because in the same breath, she said, "I have so much to tell you."

Tegan was conscious of the fact that Bailey was staring her up and down. She could feel it, like hot coals burning into every part of her. It burned worse where his boner had pressed against her.

Frogs still croaked in the starry night, but the breeze had left long ago.

CHAPTER 8

RILEIGH AND JEFF WERE all anyone talked about at school anymore.

"Gee, aren't they cute?"

"What a good couple."

"Oh, my god, I love them."

And when they weren't on the tip of everyone's tongues, Tegan and Bailey were.

"I used to see them flirt in biology, you know."

"Perfect."

"I knew it!"

What did they know? Nothing. Every time Bailey wrapped his warm, thick fingers around Tegan's, everything inside of her curdled. And when he pressed his lips against hers, in front of everyone in the hallways, it was all she could do not to dig her teeth into his flesh and tug until she'd stripped the muscle clean.

Being with Rileigh wasn't the same anymore either. The two of them barely hung out on their own. It was always double dates, which meant it was always Bailey's hand climbing up her thigh, lightly brushing against the ridge of her zipper, beneath tables.

But the boys were on different lunches, so at least Tegan had Rileigh all to herself then.

"So, guess what?" She dipped her head to the side and her hair danced across her shoulders. She'd cut it shoulder length right before summer ended, and somehow even now it looked long and powerful.

Tegan plopped her salad on the table and poured a tiny amount of dressing on. She'd read that salad was good for recovering bulimics, soft to the throat and stomach, so she'd taken to only eating salads or avocados, even though she still threw up from time to time (especially after late night phone conversations with Bailey). "Hmmm, you've finally discovered the fish monster that lives in the pond at your place?"

She waved her hand dismissively, dabbing at her pizza with a napkin with the other. "Oh, you mean Fred? We go way back. No, seriously." She leaned forward, beaming. Her eyes searched Tegan's face, urging her to pull the answer out of thin air.

Tegan took a bite of her salad and chased it down with some water. "Give me a hint."

"It's got something to do with Jeff."

Of course it does. Tegan's mood instantly soured. *Can't she go more than a few minutes without talking about him?*

"Did he propose?" Tegan flipped her right ring finger up instead of flipping Rileigh off.

Rileigh made an ugly face and threw a French fry at her. "Shithead. No, my parents are letting us go on a date alone together."

"Oh." Tegan wondered if she could puke hard enough to turn her body inside out.

Rileigh, in tune with her friend's emotions, reached across the table and wrapped her fingers around Tegan's. "We'll still go on double dates, of course. But just think of all the stories we'll have for each other!"

"Each other?"

"Well, yeah. Your dad doesn't care if you go on dates with Bailey, does he?"

"No. Not really."

"Jeff and I are going out this Saturday. You and Bailey should do something, too. Then we can stay up all night and talk on the phone about it."

I would rather have all those tubes put down my throat like my mom.

Tight, yellow skin with black craters where eyes should be. Didn't they used to shine? Hadn't she always had a beautiful smile? Where was it now? Just skin pressed tight against teeth. And she'd wanted Tegan to lay with her, but Tegan was afraid of her. Whatever was in that bed wasn't her mother anymore. It didn't look or sound or feel like her. But she'd done it, laid in a bed with bones trapped in skin. Smelled the stale breath of the walking corpse that couldn't die soon enough. Her mother had been dead long before the monitor went flat.

"Teg?"

"Hmm?" Tegan had to take a minute to refocus her eyes. She blinked a few times. "Sorry."

"You ok?"

"Yeah. Just kind of got lost in thought."

"Thinking about Bailey?" Rileigh gave her an exaggerated wink.

Tegan tried to smile, but her mouth was simply a flat line. "Oh, you know it."

"Teg, you like Bailey, don't you? You're not doing this because I asked you to, right?"

"When are we going to hang out, just the two of us? We haven't done that in forever."

They hadn't been alone in nearly two months. Hadn't been alone since Rileigh and Jeff had started dating.

Rileigh touched her hand to her heart; the other one was still holding Tegan's.

Has she really been holding my hand this whole time? A chill ran down her spine. She hated being detached from her body like that. That's why she pushed those thoughts down and threw them up later.

"You're right, it has been too long. I'm sorry. I just got so wrapped up in Jeff. And I thought that you liked hanging out with Bailey too. How about next weekend? You can come over Friday and stay until Sunday."

Tegan pulled her hand back. Her fingers were getting stiff. "Yeah sure."

Rileigh looked a bit hurt at the disconnect. "I'm sorry if I haven't been a very good friend lately, Teg. I'll try harder, ok?"

The words were empty and Tegan knew it. Everything was beginning to feel loose or too tight. Maybe she could talk her dad into moving again.

She regretted the thought as soon as it flashed into her mind. No one else in the world would glitter quite the way Rileigh could. The gold inside of Tegan's stomach turned.

She wandered through the hall in a daze. All the faces she passed were melting together. She gave a courteous nod to the people who smiled at her or said hello, but she couldn't really tell one from the other.

Strong fingers gripped her upper arm. Bruises were already forming beneath the skin. But Tegan didn't turn. She already knew who it was. And the last thing she wanted to do was see him. She wondered what would happen if she would just start screaming. Could she scream?

"I'll walk you to biology." Bailey's voice made Tegan's throat dry.

"Ok."

They walked in silence, his hand still gripping her arm, the pressure constant. Bailey said hello to a few teachers on hall duty as they passed.

Don't they see how he touches me? Don't they care? Of course, no one cares about you. What a stupid thought.

And finally, they were at the door.

"Thanks." Tegan tried to dip in front of someone and into the doorway so he couldn't grab her again, but his fingers just pressed deeper as he tugged her back.

He pursed his lips.

Vomit bubbled up in the back of Tegan's throat. She swallowed it back down out of habit.

"Kiss me."

Tegan pecked his lips hard, hard enough to hurt her front teeth. She ripped her arm out of his grip and dipped into the room.

"Love you." He smiled at her from the doorway.

Tegan hoped the look she gave him showed him all of the ice sitting within her.

He winked and disappeared.

Tegan's teeth touched. Suddenly conscious of her body she let her shoulders drop and parted her mouth to relax her jaw.

Kamryn St. Clair slipped into the chair beside her. "You and Bailey are so cute."

Visions of slamming Kamryn's head into her desk until blood pooled onto the floor helped to relax the rest of Tegan's body.

CHAPTER 9
Charlie

"YOU SURE YOU DON'T want me to walk you to your first class?" Charlie Adisa's mom called through the driver's side window. Her hand was already on the door handle.

Charlie's perfectly rounded hair bounced as she whipped around. "I'm thirteen, not five, mom. I don't need any extra help being the outcast." She held her arms out to showcase her long sleeve, black and silver dress. A studded collar rested against her dark skin.

Her mom's smile was beautiful and white, full of perfectly straight teeth. "Knock 'em dead, killer."

Charlie blew her mother a kiss before straightening her coffin shaped backpack and bursting through the doors. A few people turned around to see what the commotion was. A sea of white faces stared back at her.

She clicked her platform Doc Martens together and muttered, "There's no place like home, there's no place like home," before walking into the office.

The receptionist looked up at her from her computer.

"Oh, you must be the new girl." She reached over to a manila folder and pulled out a schedule. She slid it across the counter. "There's your schedule. Sit tight for just a minute. Rileigh will be here soon to walk you to your classes."

The idea of being led around like a dog didn't sit with Charlie too well. "No, that's fine. I think I can figure it out."

The phone rang. The receptionist rolled her eyes and pointed to a chair. "It'll be just a second." She picked up the phone and put on her fakest customer service voice. "Good morning."

Charlie looked between the receptionist and the chair. The office was like a big fish tank, glass walls closing her in for everyone to see. Kids were staring.

"Fuck this." She marched to the door, head held high.

A girl pushed through the door so quickly that she nearly knocked Charlie down. "Oh, goodness, I'm sorry. You must be

Charlie. Hi, I'm Rileigh. I'm going to walk you to your classes today."
The girl was a ray of pure sunshine. Charlie hated people who were
fake nice.

"It's cool. I think I can figure it out."

"Oh, don't be silly." Rileigh snatched Charlie's schedule from her
hands. She walked toward Charlie's locker, glancing back to see if she
followed. And begrudgingly, she did. "We have three classes together.
Well, that'll make it easier." Her blue eyes sparkled as she handed
Charlie back her schedule to crack her locker open.

"So why do you get to show me around?" Charlie dug out the
books for her first three classes.

"Oh, just because I'm nice and trustworthy." Rileigh beamed, but
there was something mischievous in her smile. She took one of
Charlie's long, hanging sleeves into her fingers. "I like this a lot.
Where'd you get it?"

Charlie snorted. "You like this?" The girl wore a bright yellow
shirt with floral print pants and hot pink ballet flats.

Rileigh looked down at herself and laughed. She pushed Charlie
playfully. "What? People can like different things, you know."

"Fair." Charlie held up her hands in defeat.

Rileigh looked her up and down. "You're so tall. Why do you
wear those big shoes?"

Charlie straightened up to reveal her full height. "Because people
don't like tall girls."

"You don't want people to like you?"

"I want people to realize they're being dipshits."

Rileigh giggled. "I like you."

"You're ok, I guess."

Rileigh bumped Charlie into one of the lockers.

***

Charlie searched the crowded cafeteria for Rileigh with no luck. They
had already had two of their three classes together and had passed the
time ignoring what was being taught to pass notes back and forth and
giggle. It turned out that the two had a lot more in common than
Charlie had initially thought. The two had filled their time talking
about books and witchcraft mostly.

All the other kids had been perfectly pleasant to her. The idea of
living in a small, white town had been causing her a lot of anxiety
lately. But so far no one had so much as given her a dirty look. And

the teachers made sure to include her in conversation, especially in her English class, but that was normal, she could talk about poetry until she passed out.

The only real problem she'd run into was the same problem she'd faced at every school— having to correct the teachers when they called her Charlotte.

"Hi, Charlie. Do you need somewhere to sit?" a tiny little girl in a Black Sabbath shirt named Leah asked. The two had met in English, one of the classes without Rileigh, and had quickly bonded over their shared love of Poe.

"Oh, hey. I was actually looking for Rileigh."

Suddenly a voice was whispering in her ear, close enough to give Charlie goosebumps. "Speak of the Devil, and he'll appear."

"Looks like you found her. Maybe next time." Leah turned her attention back to a lanky, pale boy beside her with swooped bangs.

It's a tragedy that girls like that like trash boys.

Rileigh led her to a table in the middle of the cafeteria. "Hey, Teg. This is Charlie. Charlie, this is Tegan."

The girl was small and ghostly looking. Her hair was a deep brown that hung straight to her shoulders. She was very pretty, but there was something cold about her. Something about her eyes that made her seem disconnected.

The girl waved awkwardly, looking between Charlie and Rileigh. "Nice to meet you." She drizzled dressing over her salad.

"You too." Charlie seated herself beside Rileigh, who was sitting across from Tegan.

"Tegan is my best friend. You two are going to get along great."

The girl gave Charlie a tight-lipped smile and forked some salad into her mouth.

A silence hung over the three as they ate.

"So, where are you from?" Tegan asked.

"I'm from Minneapolis."

"Oh wow."

"Yeah."

"Why move here?"

"For my mom's work."

"Did your dad find a job too?"

Charlie tore off a corner of her pizza and popped it into her mouth. She shrugged. "I don't know. I don't really have a dad."

"Tegan doesn't have a mom," Rileigh interjected.

Tegan's face turned red. The darkness that Charlie had seen behind her eyes was suddenly gone, replaced with vulnerability.

Charlie made a mental note to never tell Rileigh any of her secrets. "I'm sorry to hear that."

Tegan shrugged. "I have a really good dad at least."

"Yeah." She zoned out.

Charlie knew the hurt of losing a parent and wanted to distract Tegan from whatever reverie she had slipped into. "So, do we have any classes together?" She fished her schedule out of her bag and slid it across the table.

Tegan did not touch it, only glanced over it. "Yeah, we have our last class two classes together. You'll have the last one with me and Rileigh."

Rileigh squirmed in her seat. "I'm so excited. We always have to get into groups in that class. And now we have you." She grinned between bites of her sandwich. "You know, I think this is going to be the beginning of a beautiful friendship."

CHAPTER 10
Tegan

Her dad rapped his knuckles on the bathroom door.

Tegan had been lying half-submerged beneath the water for at least an hour. The bubbles had faded away, leaving her sitting in what looked like a tub full of diluted milk.

"What's up?"

"Bailey's on the phone for you. Can I open the door?"

Tegan let herself sink back down until her mouth was covered. She wondered how long it would take for her dad to just walk away.

Too long, apparently. He jiggled the doorknob, but Tegan had locked it before getting in. She'd found herself back in the habit of throwing up until it was just spit and bile, and she would never want to burden her dad with everything that was wrong with her.

She slid her head down so that the only thing protruding was her nose and mouth. "Give me just a second."

She lay there for a minute, listening to her heartbeat in her ears. She wished that the world would sound that way forever. She could handle a muted world.

Tegan gripped the edges of the tub and pulled herself out. She wrapped a towel around herself and cracked the door just enough to reach through and grab the phone. "Thank you."

"You doing ok, kid? You've been in there an awful long time."

"I'm sorry. I'll be out soon."

"No reason to be sorry. I just want you to know that I'm here if you need to talk."

How long would it take to drown myself? She locked the door and began to drain the tub.

"Hello?"

"We were supposed to hang out last night. What happened?" Tegan could practically feel Bailey gripping her tight enough to leave marks through the phone.

"I wasn't feeling well."

"Bullshit."

It had been weeks since she had really seen Rileigh. Sure, there had been a slumber party or two here or there, but it was always with Charlie. And it wasn't that Tegan really disliked the girl, but she wanted time to spend just with Rileigh. But that wasn't her place anymore. Charlie had taken it from her.

And Charlie usually stayed up later than Tegan as well, so she couldn't even indulge herself in the strands of gold that lay scattered across the floor. That was why they weren't close anymore. Because she wasn't able to keep a part of Rileigh with her anymore. They were losing their connection.

"Are you listening?"

Tegan lowered herself back into the water. She hadn't realized how cold it had gotten. She pushed the drain up with her foot. "No. Not really."

Bailey didn't think that was very funny. "We're going out tonight."

"I don't feel well."

"You'll feel better if you get out of the house."

No, I'll feel like dying even more outside of the house. I just won't have as many opportunities to do it with all the people watching. But wouldn't it be glorious? Forcing people to watch her die?

"I guess."

"Look, do you want me to tell everyone that you're gay for Rileigh?"

The last of the water sloshed down the drain. "I don't care anymore."

A beat of silence.

Did he believe her? Did she believer herself?

"I'll be there at six-thirty. We're going to see a movie."

Tegan hung up the phone before he could force her into telling him she loved him. She didn't know what she hated more, that or the physical contact.

Her clothes felt heavy on her. She'd lost even more weight in the past few weeks; she was probably smaller than Rileigh now. And she had none of the muscle mass that made Rileigh desirable. Just skin and bone. She lifted her shirt and twisted and contorted in front of the full-length mirror. She could make out the bones beneath the skin. She stretched the skin of her stomach flat, trying to see if she could see the thin wisps of hair beneath the surface.

Her dad was sitting on the edge of her bed when she finally managed to drag her body to her room.

He patted the bed beside him. "Sit down, kid."

She did as she was told. She was used to that now. Everything inside her was too tired to fight. "What's up?"

"What's going on?"

"What do you mean?"

"You just seem so unhappy. You barely eat anymore. You sleep all the time. Do we need to go back to the doctor?"

He had made her attend a few therapy sessions after her mother died. The therapist had been nice, but Tegan had never been able to express the things that made her stomach tight and muscles weak. How her mother had turned into a nightmare before her very eyes, and how she somehow couldn't shake the feeling of being unlovable, even though her parents had showered her in affection her entire life.

And now she was worse. What would he do to her when he found out about her relationship with Rileigh? About the hair? Would he lock her away? What about the vomiting? She was skinny enough now people might actually care about her.

"No."

He took one of her hands in his. "Talk to me. Please, Teg. I don't know what to do."

"I'm fine, Dad."

"You aren't. You never go out and do anything with your friends anymore."

"Rileigh has been hanging out with Charlie." Her voice caught in her throat. "But I'm going to the movies with Bailey tonight. If that's ok. His mom is going to pick me up, I think."

His eyes narrowed. "Is that something you want to do?"

Tegan blushed under her dad's intuitive stare. "Yes," she whispered.

"Why are you dating that boy?"

"I don't know, Dad. I like him, I guess."

He sighed. "I can't help you if I don't know what's going on."

"Nothing is going on."

"You took a bath for over an hour today. You're wasting away. I'm going to make an appointment."

"No, don't. Please." She squeezed his hand. "Everything will be ok."

"Will it?"

"I promise."

He pulled her to his chest and kissed the top of her head. "I love you, kid."

"I love you, too."
"You'll tell me if something is wrong?"
"I will."

***

Bailey's mom smiled at them from the rearview mirror.

"So nice to see you, Tegan. You should come by for dinner sometime."

Bailey squeezed her hand hard enough to grind the bones in her fingers together.

"Yeah. I will."

He released.

But Tegan didn't even bother to shake off the pain. She was used to it. At the very least it brought her out of her head. Lately, when she closed her eyes, all she could see was blood pulsing from her wrists.

She liked Bailey's mom, or, rather, she would if she wasn't his mom. She couldn't believe that someone so nice could raise someone so monstrous without knowing that something was wrong with him. Did she just ignore it? Didn't she feel bad for the girls he would hook in?

It's all fake.

She sank deeper into the seat.

"You kids have fun! Call me when you're done!"

Tegan watched the taillights disappear, even as Bailey dragged her to the ticket booth. He bought tickets to some movie Tegan could vaguely remember coming out weeks before. It didn't matter to her. She would be concentrating on keeping his hands from moving to places she didn't want them too. Which was everywhere, really, but she had to give a little leeway.

The theatre was old and filthy. Huge stains of god only knew were scattered all over the dark carpet. They passed the arcade, if you could call it that. It was a dimly lit room with a broken photobooth, two racing games, a pinball machine from a movie Tegan wasn't even sure was real, and one claw machine.

Still, there was something charming about the theatre. It used to be one of Tegan's favorite places. She didn't really have those anymore.

The walls were covered in 90's movie posters. Some were classics, others she'd never heard of. Every so often they would put a poster for a new movie up, but it would get stolen quickly.

And it smelled like butter, which Tegan enjoyed for some reason. No matter where you went in the theatre, no matter how far away from the concessions, the smell lingered.

The room was empty. Tegan's heart dropped, and she stopped at the foot of the stairs, catching Bailey off guard.

He looked back at her and tugged on her arm lightly. "Come on. We're going to the top."

"Where is everybody else?"

"Hopefully they don't come. That's why I picked this movie."

Tegan wrenched her hand out of his. "No."

"No?" For once genuine confusion was his first reaction instead of anger.

"I don't want to be alone with you. Not back there."

And the anger was back, darkening his eyes, reddening his cheeks. He tried to grab her hand, but she pulled away, shaking her head.

Rage clouded his face. Maybe more so than Tegan had ever seen him. His voice was a low whisper. "We're going to the top. Now."

Tegan looked to the door, hoping that some old person who had failed to see the movie within the first few weeks would come to her rescue. She could make out people walking by through the small window in the door, but no one stopped. No one even looked toward their theatre.

"Am I going to have to make you go up?"

Tegan still had bruises on her arm from trying to dodge him in the hall earlier that week. She didn't want anymore.

The trailers rolled on in the background.

"You go first."

Bailey's body tensed, as though he was about to stomp down the stairs and drag her up himself. But instead, he just huffed, groaned, "Fine, whatever," and trudged up the stairs.

He was already sitting, in the dead middle of the row, before Tegan had even made it to the aisle.

"Jesus, can you hurry up?" His voice was jarring in the empty room. Tegan had never heard anyone speak so loudly in a theatre.

She looked back down, hoping to see at least the face of a worker at the foot of the stairs, but there was still no one.

Tegan hovered above the seat to the right of him.

"No. Sit on the other side of me." He pulled his legs back so she could slide through.

He wrapped his fingers around hers. It was possibly the gentlest touch she'd ever received from him. He turned his body toward her, his knees pressing against hers. His face was close now, and she knew he was going to try to make her kiss him.

"What movie is this?"

He shrugged but didn't pull away. "I don't know. I think it's a comedy. Heard it wasn't any good." He inched closer.

"Then why are we seeing it?" She turned her head, though his lips were now nearly pressed onto her ear.

"Don't act stupid." He grabbed the back of her head and pulled her face to his.

Tegan let her mouth sit in a flat line, like she always did when he kissed her. But his mouth was hungrier than usual tonight. Because they were alone. Because he knew that he could get away with more, here in the dark.

His fingers pushed through her hair, digging into her scalp. She grimaced, and he took the opportunity to force his tongue into her mouth.

And her teeth came down hard, grinding back and forth, front to back. Tearing through the thick meat. Blood filled their mouths and spilled out from their lips. The warmth was welcome in the chilly theatre, and the booming action movie trailers drowned out his already muffled screams. And the harder he tried to pull away from her, the looser the flesh connecting the meat became, until finally it broke free into Tegan's mouth. Blood pulsed from his silent scream. Tegan spit the tongue back at him as she rubbed his blood all over her body, letting it soak into hers...

His tongue brushed up against her teeth, explored the side of her tongue and cheeks. The sensation made her want to gag, and she tried to pull her head back, but he pulled her closer, smashing their teeth together.

Did she taste blood?

She pushed against his chest, but his tongue only went deeper in response. She couldn't fight the sensation anymore. She began to shake and retch.

He pulled away. "What the fuck?"

Tegan covered her mouth, but nothing was coming. The bile rose halfway up her throat but slid back down as she swallowed.

"I don't like that."

He slammed himself back into the chair and crossed his arms. "Why are you so fucking weird?"

The movie had already started. And they were still alone. Tegan wondered what Bailey would do if she simply burst into tears. She felt it, right there on the edge. She held her face to keep her chin from trembling.

She sat like that for some time, on the edge of her seat, holding her chin with her eyes closed. She would have sat like that for the whole movie if Bailey wouldn't have said, "Can you stop being a fucking freak? Sit back."

She let herself fall back but didn't release her face.

"Stop that shit." Bailey wrenched her hands free.

Tegan shivered. Her body was crying but no tears were falling. She wrapped her arms around herself to stop it.

Bailey stroked her knee.

Would he stop if I puked on him?

His hand traveled further up her thigh. She pushed it away. She didn't care how many bruises that would get her. She never wanted to be touched that way. Not by anyone.

He grabbed her hand and Tegan wondered if he was finally going to really hit her, if he was just opening a good shot to her face. She would have preferred that. He placed her hand in his lap, at the top of his thigh, and removed his hand.

She kept it there for a few minutes, hoping this would satisfy him, then picked it up. He pushed it back down.

He clenched his fingers around hers, pushing them into the meat of his thigh. The tip of his penis brushed against her knuckles.

She froze. She could neither find the energy, or nerve, to pull away or dig her nails into him.

This is exactly what you deserve. This is normal, you freak. You should like this.

The sound of him undoing his zipper shook but did not move her.

This is happening.

Some part of her hated herself for not fighting back. But how could she? He was so much stronger. And shouldn't it be flattering? To get this kind of attention? Why didn't she want it? What was wrong with her?

He moved her hand up, up, up—

And filled her open hand with it. It was warm and thicker than she could have thought.

Vomit poured from her mouth in a stream.

"Ugh, what the fuck!"

She caught a glimpse of it before he could shove it back into his pants. He gagged at the sight of her vomit dripping down his leg.

Tegan hoped he would hit her. She deserved it.

"I'm calling my mom." He stomped down the stairs.

Speckles of her vomit were illuminated in the light of the movie as the scene changed.

Someone's going to have to clean that.

CHAPTER 11

"ARE YOU MAD AT me?"

"Huh?" Tegan hadn't even noticed that Rileigh had sat beside her. *How long has she been there?* She dropped the piece of pizza she'd been absentmindedly picking at.

"Why would I be mad at you?"

"Look, Teg, I know I've been spending a lot of time with Charlie lately, but you're still my very best friend. Ok?" Tegan had never seen Rileigh look so genuinely concerned.

Maybe she really does care. No. If she did, she would save you from Bailey. She wouldn't have made you be with him in the first place. She wouldn't have replaced you.

"Ok." She rose as the bell rang and dumped her food, still intact save for a few tiny pieces torn off of the square school pizza, and pushed through the crowd to get to the door.

Rileigh's fingers gripped her arm. They pressed into Bailey's bruises, but her touch was softer, afraid rather than aggressive.

Tegan pulled away. "What?"

"Please forgive me. I'm worried about you, Teg. So is Charlie. So are a lot of people. You haven't been the same lately."

Didn't she care that the people around them could hear? Wouldn't she know that it would be embarrassing to Tegan to have everyone at the school know something was wrong? To have their eyes on her, to occupy their thoughts, be brought up in their conversations?

"I don't know what you're talking about."

Rileigh cupped Tegan's face in her hands. "Come dress shopping with us for spring formal. Then you can stay the night, like old times."

"With you and Charlie?" Tegan wanted so badly to bask in Rileigh's soft touch, but she'd hurt her. She was undeserving of her love and touch. Her throat tightened, and her chin trembled. Hot tears clung to her eyelashes. She wiped them aggressively.

Rileigh blinked in confusion. She thought that was how friendship worked, all of them together all the time. But she had been spending a lot of time alone with Charlie and none with Tegan. But Tegan had seemed so wrapped up in Bailey. She hadn't meant to hurt her. "We'll all go dress shopping together and then we'll go back to my place. Just me and you. Ok?"

"You don't have to do that." Tegan tilted her head back to contain the tears.

"I know. I want to. I love you. And I miss you. I'm sorry I've been a shitty friend. I just thought you would want some time with Bailey. But I focused too much of my time on Jeff and Charlie, and I really am sorry, Teg. Can you forgive me?"

Rileigh's hair brushed against Tegan's face as she embraced her. Instead of fighting it, she leaned in this time, smelling the rose petal shampoo, feeling the gold tickle her skin. This was where she belonged, wrapped in a waterfall of blonde hair.

"I forgive you."

"Yeah? So you'll come?"

"Yes."

"Friday right after school. My mom will pick us up and take us."

Tegan expected Rileigh to leave after her little explanation, but instead she intertwined their fingers and walked Tegan to class.

Bailey watched from the end of the hall, clenching and unclenching his fist.

And for the first time in what seemed like a very long time, Tegan felt safe and at least somewhat happy again.

***

"I'm coming." Bailey had hit yet another growth spurt and towered over the rest of the kids in the hallway. His newfound height brought newfound strength, and he'd left a hand-shaped bruise on Tegan's hip from grabbing her.

Tegan had tried to wait until the last minute to tell Bailey that she was spending the weekend with Rileigh, and she would be picking out her dress with her and Charlie, but once he'd seen the two girls talking in the hall he wouldn't leave her alone about it.

"No, you aren't. Girls pick out their dresses together."

"No. We should pick out your dress together, because I'll have to work with whatever color you pick. And you're not picking something fucking ugly. Or slutty."

The bright side of his growth spurt was that he now had to awkwardly hunch down to reach for Tegan's hand. She let someone walk between them when he reached.

Rileigh was at the end of the hall, waiting by the double doors that led to freedom. The cold winter sun illuminated her smile. She waved.

"Hey, Teg!"

Tegan sped up her pace until her arms were wrapped around Rileigh.

Charlie popped her head around the doorframe and waved.

"Hi, Charlie." Tegan's heart sank a little at the sight of her. She was too cool for Tegan to compete with, but also so unlike Rileigh that she couldn't imagine how the two got along.

Charlie smiled at her, then looked Bailey up and down. She seemed unimpressed and let her attention wander back outside.

"Where are you guys going?" Bailey demanded.

Rileigh grinned. "It's a secret."

Charlie popped her head back into the doorframe. "Yeah, no boys allowed."

Bailey sneered at her. "I wasn't talking to you."

"Oh, but I was talking to you though." Charlie didn't even turn around to look at him.

Tegan had to bite her cheeks to keep from bursting into laughter. *Maybe Charlie isn't so bad after all.*

Rileigh's mom honked from the pickup line.

Rileigh wrapped an arm around Tegan's waist and pulled her toward the door. "See ya later, Bailey."

Tegan exchanged pleasantries with Rileigh's mom ("It's been too long! How's your father?") as she watched Bailey fade into the distance, clenching and unclenching his fists.

***

Charlie refused to take her dress off after she found it. "I'll just wear it until you guys are done." She twirled in front of the mirror, tracing a hand over her curveless body. It was a black lace dress with long sleeves that hung low like something you'd see a witch wear and ended above her knees. She hadn't removed her black combat boots, and had declared that this was exactly what she would wear to the actual event.

Rileigh's mom had left them to wander around herself; she was good about that, leaving them alone.

Now was Rileigh's turn. While Charlie had immediately found her dress, and seemingly just tried it on to be able to be in it for a little longer, Rileigh was taking forever. She had already gone through five dresses.

"It has to be perfect," she'd said as she pouted at a clingy, little yellow thing that obviously wasn't going to make the cut.

Tegan couldn't picture her in anything but a big, pink, puffy prom dress, like something you'd see in an old 80's movie.

Rileigh disappeared back into the changing room, where ten more dresses hung, ready to be tossed to the side. Tegan had a handful of dresses herself, but the idea of coming out and modeling them made her want to melt. She knew that certain things looked better on different people with different body types, but she also just wore things that fit, whether they were flattering or not. No matter what she wore she was disgusted with the way she looked. She thought that losing weight would fix that, but it hadn't.

"What do you even see in that dude?"

"Huh?" Tegan was so deep in her own thoughts that she had kind of forgotten that Charlie was sitting beside her.

"Bailey. Why do you date him?" Her eyes were cold and judgmental.

Tegan shrugged. "I don't know."

"Then why not dump him?"

She shrugged again, running a hand through her hair. A fistful of strands stayed trapped in her fingers. She shook them off.

Charlie reached over and grabbed Tegan's hands. Tegan nearly screamed. She hadn't felt a nice touch in so long from anyone but her dad, not that she would have accepted a kind gesture from someone she barely knew anyway, but she suddenly realized how accustomed she had grown to being bruised and grabbed.

"Don't stay with someone who makes you unhappy." Charlie's big brown eyes were soft now. She reminded Tegan of a fawn, beautiful and wispy. "You're a great girl. You can do so much better than that sack of shit."

But I don't want anyone. You're all making me do this.

Tegan couldn't stop her bottom lip from trembling, and against her will she found herself squeezing Charlie's hands, too. She sniffed and tossed her head back, trying to hold back the tears that were exhausting her mind and body.

The dressing room door burst open. "Guys, I think this is it." Rileigh beamed and gave a twirl.

Tegan ripped her hands away from Charlie so violently that Charlie almost spilled into the floor at her feet.

Rileigh blinked at the two. "Is everything ok?"

Of course, everything was ok. Rileigh looked heavenly in a short, white dress with lace flowers swirled throughout, reminiscent of something you'd see a fashionista wear in the 60's.

"Fine. Everything's fine." Tegan said the words so quickly that she wasn't even sure they'd understood her. "Great dress."

Rileigh looked shell-shocked. She turned to Charlie for answers, but Charlie looked back to Tegan, whose wild eyes resembled those of a cornered animal.

"Yeah. Everything is fine. We'll be total opposites. What kind of shoes are you thinking of wearing?"

Rileigh, always pleased to have the topic of conversation turned to her, flattened the dress against herself, peaked a foot forward and shrugged. "I'm not sure. What do you think? Maybe a nice wood wedge?"

Now that attention had been taken off Tegan, she could finally bring herself back down. Her body warmed, from her face to her fingertips. She hated Charlie. Why would she say that here? Where people could see and hear? Where everyone would know that something was wrong with her—that she was entertaining a fake relationship to just try to smash herself into an idea of normalcy. She bit the insides of her lips hard enough to draw blood. The taste of copper filled her mouth. She swallowed it.

Rileigh scooped her remaining dresses up in her arms and tossed them on the return rack. She started to unzip her dress before the door even closed.

Charlie reached over to hold Tegan again, but she pulled back, clenching her hands tightly so there was no way for Charlie to wiggle her fingers between them.

"Stop," Tegan hissed.

Charlie blinked at her, then straightened. "What's wrong?"

"Just leave me alone." The tears were beginning to well up again, which just made Tegan more upset. She wanted to smack herself until they stopped, and dig her fingers into her eyes until there was nothing to cry but blood.

"I wasn't trying to make you upset. I just want to help you."

"If you want to help me just leave me alone."

Charlie opened her mouth to reply but clamped it shut instead. She held her hands up in defeat. "Whatever you want."

Tegan slid past Rileigh and into the room. She hung her dresses on the hook and stared at herself in the full-length mirror.

She'd been avoiding mirrors for a while now, and she was thankful that she had. Her eyes were red rimmed and unfocused, her cheekbones were sharp and too deep, her collar bones protruded, and her skin was like yellow paper stretched thin.

She never thought that she would hate her skinny body as much as she had hated her fat one.

She turned her back on the mirror and grabbed a strapless plum dress. She tugged off her sweater and slid out of her jeans.

She looked down at herself in admiration. The plum looked beautiful against her pale skin, and it clung to her body without being too tight or exposing. The material was smooth and silky, and if she moved a certain way, the light would catch it and make it look as though it were a shimmering pool of darkness.

The joy for her was fleeting.

As she reached for the door handle, she decided to steal a glance of herself in the mirror. Her arms were covered in bruises of all hues. Some had shrunk in size, but there was no way anyone could not recognize that they were fingerprints.

A cold wave washed through her and made her organs seize for a moment. How had she not known how bad it had gotten?

Because he has been slowly getting worse, boiling me like a frog.

Her stomach hitched like she wanted to vomit. A sharp pain ripped through the right side of her abdomen. She groaned and clutched it.

The dress was perfect. She was what was wrong. She let herself slide back down onto the little bench and squeezed her eyes shut tightly.

My skin looks like how my mother's looked before she died. I'm dried up. I'm dying. They're going to put me in a room until I am not myself, just a husk, and let the people come look at me and pretend that they cared.

A knock on the door.

"Teg? You ok in there?" Rileigh's voice broke through Tegan's thoughts of her mother.

"Yeah, I'm fine."

A beat.

"You gonna come out and show us your dress?"

"I don't think so. I like it. I'm gonna get it." She was already starting to pull an arm out.

"Come on, show us! You've got to." Rileigh was excited to swoon over her friend, to build her self-esteem and try to get her to love herself as much as she did.

"No, it's fine. It'll be a surprise." But her voice caught in her throat.

Why am I crying?

The doorknob jiggled. "Hey. Let us in." It was Charlie.

Tegan rushed to the corner of the room, trapped. They couldn't open the door unless she let them. But the knob continued to jiggle.

"Please let us in. Please," Rileigh begged.

Is that noise... me? Tegan wiped the tears off her face and tried to stifle her breathing.

"We just want to help you," Charlie pleaded.

Fine. If they want to see me like this, to see what a monster I've become, they can. Then they can leave me alone forever and I can finally kill myself. Slit my wrists and sink into the tub. But, no. Dad would find me. I could hang myself in the woods. Leave a note for him.

The door was opened, Tegan filled its frame. She held her arms out wide, rotating them so that the girls could get a better glimpse of her bruises.

The tears were still pouring. Faster now, rushing down her neck.

All she wanted was for Rileigh to wrap her arms around her, and comfort her in a halo of hair. But she was pressed into Charlie's chest before she really had the chance to process anything. And she was holding her back, pressing her fingers into Charlie's back hard enough to feel her spine, greedy for a good touch.

Charlie rubbed her hair. "Shh. It's ok."

But it wasn't ok. It hadn't been ok in a long time and Tegan wasn't sure that it ever really would be. Not in the way it was for other people.

"What happened?" Rileigh's voice was barely a whisper.

Charlie formed the name that Tegan didn't have the strength to. "Bailey."

Tegan could feel all the eyes in the store staring at her, so she held her breath for a few seconds, stopping the shaking sobs that wracked her body. She finally managed to pull herself away from Charlie's chest, ready to confront all the eyes, ready to be pitied by all.

But no one was looking. No one was even around, but she was sure that everyone in the store had heard her. She struggled to wipe her eyes. Charlie didn't let her go.

"Is that true, Teg? Did Bailey do this to you?" Rileigh cupped Tegan's face in her hand.

Tegan told them everything—from the night where Rileigh and Jeff left them, to the incident in the theatre.

"Why didn't you tell us?" Charlie asked.

"I was embarrassed." Tegan wasn't really that worried about what Charlie would think of her. Not then, or now, but the idea of Rileigh disbelieving her, spurning her because Bailey was friends with her boyfriend was what had really kept her quiet. She could lose Rileigh. Even though she already had a long time ago, that night with Jeff, then again when Charlie came.

Rileigh wrapped her arms tight around Tegan and kissed her temple. "Don't ever be afraid to tell me anything, ok? I love you, you're my best friend. I should have noticed that something was wrong. Charlie kept telling me that something seemed off, but I just didn't listen."

Charlie thinks about me?

"He's a piece of shit." Charlie shrugged. It was a simple fact to her.

Rileigh nodded. She held Tegan back at arm's length and looked her up and down. "Well, black, white, and purple do kind of go together."

Tegan looked down at her bruises.

"We can just go to the dance together," Rileigh clarified. "Charlie, do you have a date?"

"Nope. I was just gonna hang out with you guys." She beamed at Tegan.

"But what about Jeff?"

Rileigh shrugged. "He'll understand."

CHAPTER 12

RILEIGH PACED AROUND HER room, phone glued to the side of her head. "What do you mean you don't believe it?"

She paused her mini-rampage to listen. Tegan could hear Jeff yelling through the phone, though she couldn't make out what he was saying.

Rileigh looked at Tegan in disgust. She was glad she couldn't hear him.

"Are you kidding me?"

A pause as she listened. She laughed, but it was short and cruel.

"Fine then." She hung the phone up and tossed it onto her bed.

She continued to pace around the room for a bit, occasionally opening her mouth like she was going to start a conversation, then snapping it closed so hard that Tegan could swear she heard her teeth clank.

Finally, she collapsed on the bed beside Tegan. "Did you hear that shit?"

"Not really."

"He told me we would break up if I didn't go to the dance with him because he didn't believe you." She looked as though that was the stupidest thing anyone could have said. "Like, are you fucking kidding me?"

Tegan blinked at hearing Rileigh utter "fuck." She'd been spending too much time with Charlie.

The phone vibrated across the bed sheets. Rileigh ignored the call, then turned the phone off.

A wave of guilt was drowning Tegan already, even though this was the happiest outcome she could have ever dreamed up. "You can go with him."

Rileigh looked at her as though she had slapped her. "No way. I don't want anything to do with someone who's friends with someone like that. That's basically giving your approval for that stuff, you know?" She bounded back up, back to her pacing. "You know what he said, Teg?"

She shook her head, but that didn't seem to appease Rileigh, so she answered, "No."

"He said he didn't think Bailey would do something like that. That he's never showed any signs of being abusive. Has he never seen the way he touches you? How he kept you from talking to other people?"

If she noticed all these things, why didn't she say something? Why didn't she try to spend more time with her?

Tegan couldn't control herself. "But you weren't talking to me either."

Rileigh deflated. "I know. And I'm sorry. I was just caught up in having a relationship and making a new friend. That won't happen again, ok? I won't ever let anything come between us again."

Tegan wasn't sure she believed her, but even if she was lying it was still nice to hear. "All right."

Now that Rileigh was sure that she'd talked away Tegan's emotions she was back on her tirade. "I mean, seriously. What the hell is his problem? He's going to break up with me?" She laughed. It was hard and bitter.

But Tegan just nodded and let her carry on.

Once she'd worn herself out, she flopped down on the bed beside Tegan. She wiggled her hand beneath Tegan's and intertwined their fingers.

Tegan's stomach tightened. A sharp pain pulsed through her from her abdomen to her legs. She wrapped her free arm around her torso and bent forward. And she knew it was crazy, but she thought that she felt a tight ball beneath her skin.

"What's wrong?"

"I don't know. Just a stomachache." She didn't let go of Rileigh's hand, and little by little, the pain began to fade.

"What do you want to do?" Rileigh began to trace small circles on the back of Tegan's hand.

The ball in her stomach seemed to jump up to her throat. "Can I braid your hair?"

Rileigh's face lit up. She sat up quickly, her hair swinging across her shoulders and covering her face from the force. "Of course! I love when people play with my hair. I used to make my mom comb my hair every night. She hasn't done it in forever though." She rushed to her vanity and grabbed her brush.

She plopped down on the bed, back turned to Tegan.

The knot in Tegan's stomach expanded. She stretched her fingers out across the tight skin and could have sworn that she felt tendrils moving beneath the flesh.

Her hair had no tangles, and the brush ran through it smooth like moving through a cloud or body of water. She lost herself in the motions, back and forth, side to side, and tried her hardest not to touch it with her fingers, unsure if she would be able to stop once she started.

Her fingers ran against the grain, pushing from the base of Rileigh's skull to the top of her head. Her fingers gripped, feeling the strands push through the space between them, dragging against Rileigh's scalp. And then she pulled and pulled. And she kept pulling until it was free, and it was hers. And there was no blood and no pain, and when she forced the hair into her mouth there was only pleasure.

"Can you braid?"

"Hmm?"

Rileigh pulled the brush out of Tegan's hand. "Braid."

Tegan wasn't sure if she was repeating for her understanding or if it was a command.

Her fingers shook as she ran her fingers through the resplendent locks. It was like an electric shock ran through her fingertips, reaching deep inside her body, all the way down the middle of her. Her nipples hardened. She realized she was holding her breath and tried to exhale as quietly as possible.

She'd never braided hair before, but from her understanding it wasn't very hard. Just weave the hair together without tangling it. And angel hair didn't tangle anyway.

"I really am sorry that I ignored you. I didn't mean to."

"I know." Tegan wished she'd be quiet so she could concentrate on the shiver that was rushing through her body.

Silence.

"You really don't like boys?"

"I really don't."

"Oh."

Strands of hair pulled loose in Tegan's hands. She shook them loose onto her clothes, hoping that they would cling.

"Do you think you like girls?" Rileigh's voice was strained.

"No. I don't like anyone. Not like that."

Rileigh scrunched her face, as though this idea was too hard to process. But finally, she just shrugged. "All right."

Tegan didn't want to finish the knot at the end of the gold cord, but it came quickly with Rileigh's shorter hair. "Do you want me to tie this or let it loose?"

Rileigh removed a hair tie from her wrist and handed it back. She ran her fingers over it and glanced at it in the mirror. She smiled. "Pretty."

She scooted back up to the top of the bed and burrowed beneath the covers. "Will you turn off the light?"

Tegan obeyed, eyeing the strands of hair she had caught before she was plunged into darkness.

"Rileigh?" Tegan asked to the dark ceiling.

"Hmm?"

"You promise we'll be together more now?"

"I promise."

Tegan settled back into her pillow.

After Rileigh's breathing had deepened, she ran her fingers up and down her shirt and shoveled the gold into her mouth.

The knot inside her stomach twitched.

CHAPTER 13

TEGAN HAD BEEN LOCKED in the bathroom for nearly an hour under the pretense of getting ready for Rileigh's birthday party. In reality, she had been examining her emaciated looking body in the mirror, pressing her fingers against her bones. When she sucked her stomach in, she could see a hard, softball sized mass beneath the surface of her skin.

The ball flattened when she touched it, snaking out in different directions.

She forced her fingers down her throat over and over, but nothing but water came up between her dry heaving.

Her dad rapped on the door. "You still getting ready, kid?"

Tegan wiped her eyes, wet from coughing, and tugged her swimsuit on. "I'm almost done. Getting dressed now."

"All right." He didn't leave. "You excited for the party?"

Tegan pulled a pair of shorts on, and her school spirit shirt, before wrangling her hair back into a ponytail.

"Yeah. I guess," she said as she opened the door and pushed past him.

Her dad followed her down the stairs. "How's Rileigh been? Haven't seen her in a little while."

Tegan shrugged, grabbing her overnight bag from the couch. Rain was hammering against the windows. Rileigh's family had rented out an indoor swimming pool this year due to the storms that had rolled through.

"It's heated!" Rileigh had exclaimed to anyone who would listen.

The two of them ran to the truck. They were soaked by the time they closed the doors.

"Jeez, it's really coming down, huh?" Her dad waited for the windshield to clear up before putting the truck into reverse.

"Yeah."

"Are the sessions getting any better?"

He had made her go back to therapy after her relationship with Bailey had ended. It was impossible for her to keep anything from him, so when he'd asked, she'd crumbled and showed him all the bruises.

He was constantly worried about her it seemed. "Are you getting enough sleep? You look so tired all the time." "Why aren't you eating more?" "You sleep too much. You sure you don't want to go out and do anything?" "You don't seem like yourself anymore."

He'd instated a strict rule that she was to drink at least one PediaSure a day. He would corral her in the kitchen and watch her drink the entire thing, no matter how long it took. The knot in her stomach had made it nearly impossible to eat anymore.

She, too. had noticed that she didn't seem like herself anymore. The pain that she had always carried within her had shifted to anger somewhere along the way. Every time she tried to sleep, she imagined herself absorbing other people, pulling them in and suffocating them. Becoming them, until she was no longer her at all.

She was unsure of how long it had been since she'd really been able to eat or use the bathroom properly. A pain shot out from the knot in her stomach anytime she tried. The pain was sharp enough to double her over sometimes. She didn't really have the urge to vomit anymore, either. But, then again, she didn't feel anxious like she'd used to anymore. The anxiety had been replaced by nothingness. She could no longer see a future in front of her, and she often wished she just didn't wake up anymore. It wouldn't really change anything. There wasn't an urge to kill herself, just a desire to not be alive anymore.

The truck lurched to a stop.

"Well, kid, you want me to walk you in?"

Tegan watched the other kids go in. None of them went with their parents. She shrugged.

"I guess not."

"Yeah, wouldn't want to embarrass you."

"You don't embarrass me." She reached over and squeezed his hand. Then, overcome by a sudden burst of sadness and love for him, scooted across the seat and wrapped her arms around him. They stayed like that for a bit, listening to the rain while they held one another, then Tegan kissed her dad's cheek and said, "I love you. More than anything or anyone."

The large man's eyes began to water a little. "I love you too, kiddo."

We're never going to see each other again.

"I'll see you tomorrow." She pulled her hood up and ran to the doors.

She was greeted by the nearly nauseating smell of chlorine.

"Hello, sweetheart." Rileigh's mother pulled her in for a hug. She pointed to a door on the other side of the pool, which was already filled with kids. "The locker room is over there. Just drop your stuff off and go ahead and get in the pool." She went back to setting up a table of food and snacks.

Rileigh and Charlie were standing by the locker room with Rileigh's dad. A teenage boy, not much older than them, but certainly in high school, was showing him where the cleaning solutions were in case anything were to happen.

Charlie was practically drooling over him.

"Tegan! You're just gonna try to sneak by without even saying hi?" Rileigh pulled her into a hug.

Tegan patted her arm. "Was just trying to hurry up and get in the pool." The crowd for her party was quite a bit smaller than usual. Tegan assumed it had something to do with the storms. "Where is everybody?"

"Oh, I only invited the best of the best this year." She winked. Her eyes searched Tegan's face for even the trace of a smile, but Tegan couldn't muster one. "I thought you'd be here earlier."

"I figured Charlie would be helping you."

"That doesn't mean you couldn't help."

Tegan shrugged. "My dad wanted to wait out some of the rain. Didn't work."

Rileigh picked up a strand of Tegan's soaking hair. "I see that."

Tegan didn't know what else to say. "I'm going to get dressed. See you in a minute."

Rileigh followed her. "Well, I can keep you company."

"If you want."

Charlie was too preoccupied attempting to flirt to follow along.

The locker room was eerie. Nearly half of the lights were out. "Trying to save power?" Tegan joked.

"Oh, no. Just a piece of shit." Rileigh plopped down on a bench beside the locker Tegan picked. "You haven't been answering the phone lately."

"Yeah. I just haven't been feeling very well."

"Are you ok?"

"I think so. Just a little under the weather." Tegan began to strip.

"I've been trying to get you to come over all week."

"I knew I'd see you today."

"Yeah, but I want to see you more. Like it used to be. We can do things as a group—me, you, and Charlie—and then we can do things just me and you."

"Sure."

Rileigh shifted uncomfortably. She wasn't used to Tegan not wanting her attention.

But Tegan hadn't noticed. She'd finished pulling on her swimsuit during their exchange and was in the process of pulling her hair back into a tight, high ponytail.

Rileigh looked her up and down. She put one hand on either side of her small frame. "Teg. You've gotten so tiny."

"Oh. Yeah."

"You look great."

I look like I'm dying. I look like my mother when she died. But skinny is beautiful, no matter how damaging.

She gave her a skeletal smile. "Thanks. You too."

Rileigh, seemingly satisfied in thinking she'd won Tegan back over, interlaced their fingers and pulled her from the room. She pushed her onto the diving board and rushed up to meet her.

"Cannonball?"

It wasn't really a question. That's what they would be doing. But Tegan didn't mind. For the first time in weeks, she wasn't in pain as she dropped into the water, hand clasped around Rileigh's.

***

Rileigh clung to Tegan's side throughout the night.

I should have stopped caring about life earlier.

"You have our number if anything happens," Rileigh's mother had said as she locked the door behind her, locking the girls in the pool.

They swam for a little while longer, and ate some extra cake, but they were all effectively worn out not too long after.

They lay on the floor together in rows, close beside one another. Rileigh positioned herself between Tegan and Charlie. Charlie had occupied her time with the other girls, and Tegan was thankful for it.

But it wasn't long before the knot in her stomach began to stretch again. Pain enveloped her torso, making it hard for her to breathe, but she pretended to sleep, hoping that no one would notice the way her body contorted beneath her blanket.

"Rileigh," Charlie whispered. "Are you still up?"

"Yeah."

"Smoke?"

Tegan's eyes nearly popped open. Smoking? Rileigh?

"Where?"

"There's a window in the locker room. We'll just need to drag a chair over to it." Charlie rose from her spot.

Tegan squeezed her eyes together tightly. The pain was spreading down her legs.

"I need it. Been around too many people today." Rileigh and Charlie's footsteps got further and further away.

She was with me all day. Is my presence really that exhausting?

The pain got sharper throughout her back and she spasmed on the floor. She sucked in a deep breath and curled up into a ball.

The soft glow from the pool lights illuminated tiny slivers on the floor. At first Tegan thought they were bugs stretching out to her. She jolted up, but nearly fell face first from the pressure in her stomach.

Hair. Strands of wet hair covered the floor.

Eat it. Eat it. Eat it.

The voice inside her head wasn't her own. But it was telling her that eating the hair was the only way to stop the pain.

Just a little more pain, then you'll be what you've always wanted.

She scooted away from the other girls and crawled on her hands and knees, scooping up the hair and pushing it between her lips until her cheeks were stuffed.

CHAPTER 14
Charlie

"I'M WORRIED ABOUT HER." Charlie blew a plume of smoke out of the cracked open window. Strands of her tightly curled hair reached out the window.

Rileigh held her hand out, and the two swapped places. Rileigh took a drag off their shared cigarette. Charlie had started smoking right when she turned thirteen due to hanging out with some older kids. She hadn't wanted to get Rileigh started, but she had insisted.

"At least she came tonight. I would have been a lot more worried if she wouldn't have come." Rileigh had to stand on her tiptoes, even on the chair, to push her smoke out the window.

Charlie leaned against the wall, but it was slightly wet and she pulled away with a groan. The only openable window that she could find was the one in the back of the showers.

"I just don't think she's been really doing ok since the Bailey stuff."

"That was months ago."

"Yeah, but that shit will fuck you up, you know?" Charlie couldn't understand why she seemed to care about Tegan more than Rileigh did. They were supposed to be best friends after all. But Rileigh had a way of only caring about something if it affected her.

Rileigh took another drag. "Yeah, I know." Smoke pushed through her lips slightly. "I don't know. She seemed fine last time we hung out."

"Didn't you notice how thin she'd gotten, though?"

"Yeah. I told her she looks great." She lowered herself from the chair and handed the remainder of the cigarette off to Charlie.

Charlie took a deep inhale. Blew it out. "No, dude. She looks sick."

Finally, Rileigh looked concerned. Charlie could see her brow furrowing in the rays of moonlight that spilled down on her. She sucked on her bottom lip. "Yeah. She is pretty small. I don't know. What could we even do?"

"Maybe talk to her Dad?"

"That feels too much like tattling."

Charlie shrugged. She didn't care if someone didn't like her if she was helping them in the long run. Some people couldn't accept help. "You should do it anyway. I'll do it with you."

"She's in therapy again, I know."

Charlie flicked the butt out the window and cranked it close. "Well, that's good at least."

Rileigh walked the chair back to its rightful place at the end of a row of lockers, then dug through hers and spritzed herself with body spray. She offered the little bottle to Charlie.

Charlie sprayed herself a few times, even though she knew the smell of the chlorine would eventually drown out the smokey smell. She couldn't stop thinking about how she could see the notches in Tegan's spine through her bathing suit. Or how her hair seemed thinner, and her skin almost seemed yellow.

Rileigh straightened up and took a step toward the door.

"You just gonna leave me?"

"Shh." She held up a hand and looked to the door like a pointer. "Did you hear that?"

Charlie paused. She tossed the bottle back into the locker and closed it gently. "Hear what?"

"Shut up!" Rileigh hissed.

And now Charlie could hear...something. It sounded like someone gagging almost. Then she heard the cries of the other girls.

Rileigh looked at her in shock before bolting out the door. Charlie was quick behind.

It was hard to tell what was really going on. The only lights came from the ones inside the pool. All Charlie could tell was that someone was crawling around along the edge of the pool and the rest of the girls were scrambling to get away from her. Charlie knew that it had to be one of the other girls, but in the darkness, from how far away she was, it looked like some spiny creature dragging themselves around.

It's Tegan.

"What is she doing?" One of the girls screamed.

"She's eating the hair!" another cried. A few of the girls were gagging.

Charlie didn't even really process she was moving toward the others until she was nearly close enough to touch them. Rileigh was right beside her.

Tegan was shoveling loose strands of hair into her mouth, eyes rolled back, tears streaming down her face.

"Tegan. What are you doing?" Rileigh gasped.

Tegan's eyes rolled forward and focused on Rileigh. Slowly, she rose, but she doubled over just as she stretched her body out, grabbing at her stomach. "It won't stop," she sobbed. She reached a hand out and stumbled forward. Charlie moved to help her, but Rileigh pulled her back.

"You're a fucking freak," Amanda Higgins hissed. "I'm calling my mom. I'm not staying in here with her."

A few of the girls nodded in agreement.

Even in the dim glow of the pool lights Charlie could see that Rileigh's face was pink.

"No." Rileigh's voice was harsh and cold. "She can go."

Tegan dropped to her knees again, clutching her stomach. She gasped and began to heave. "Please," she cried between sobs and gags. "Rileigh, please." She crawled forward. The girls backed up.

Charlie reached out to her, but Tegan pulled her hand away.

Her whole body convulsed. Her face contorted in horrific ways in the low light.

Charlie stumbled backward. "Someone call somebody!"

But the girls were rooted where they stood, watching Tegan seize and foam at the mouth. Then, she was still.

Charlie felt someone pulling her back.

"Oh my God," Rileigh whispered.

Charlie felt disconnected from her body. Every breath she took felt as though she was trying to breathe herself out of her skin. Out and gone, like Tegan. And they had all just stood there and watched her die.

But now she could breathe again, and her fingertips were tingling. She squeezed her hands shut tightly. And she could feel that the hands that had pulled her back were still digging into her arms.

She pulled away from Rileigh violently, nearly knocking her into the pool. "Don't fucking touch me!"

Rileigh blinked in confusion, tears in her eyes. She reached for her again. "Charlie, please."

"No." Charlie pushed past her, heading to the locker room. *I have to call someone. Have to get out of here. Can't handle this. Can't handle these people.*

One of the girls gasped. "Look!"

Charlie, already halfway to the locker room, turned back.

Tegan wasn't dead after all. She had crawled back onto her hands and knees and was staring up at the group of girls before her. Staring at Rileigh.

She opened her mouth as though to say something, but it wasn't words that came out, it was long strands of hair. The hair slithered from her mouth like snakes, writhing on the floor.

The girls screamed. Some of them ran past Charlie, but a few were glued where they stood in shock and terror.

More hair rushed from Tegan's open mouth, but now it was coming from other places as well. It escaped from her nose and ears. Her eyes gave way, exploding from her face and landing on the floor with a sickening *splat!*

Charlie felt lightheaded.

Finally, all the girls managed to tear themselves away from where they stood. Except Amanda, who watched in terror as Tegan's body stretched and groaned before popping like a balloon, showering her in chunks of flesh and blood. She didn't even scream.

But Charlie did. And she began to scream Amanda's name as the bloody hair piled itself up, higher and higher, until it stood at about Amanda's height. Piss splashed on the floor as Amanda finally got the nerve to run.

But it was too late. The hair dove for Amanda's head, grasping at the end of her ponytail. The force dropped her to her knees, and she would have fallen face first if it wouldn't have been for the hair monster tearing at Amanda's locks. Blood began to drip down Amanda's face as her scalp came loose, joining the mound of hair.

She dropped to the ground screaming, but as the hair advanced over her, it stopped.

Charlie nearly fell back on her ass at the force of Rileigh pulling her.

"Come on!" Rileigh's voice broke through the ringing in Charlie's ears.

The monster, Tegan, moved toward them at the sound of Rileigh's voice, leaving wet wiggling strands in its wake.

Charlie sprinted to the locker room, passing Rileigh as she ran. The door didn't budge. She pounded on it. "Let us in!"

The door opened just wide enough for them to squeeze through. The other girls were crying, and a few were frantically trying to find a signal to call their parents.

Rileigh locked the door and backed away. "The window," she said to Charlie.

Charlie shook her head. "We can't fit through that. It's too small." She watched the crack beneath the door, afraid she would see movement. "We have to get out of here."

"We can't. The doors are locked, remember?"

"Your parents didn't leave you an extra key or anything?"

Rileigh shook her head.

"Fuck." Charlie gripped her hair, but the sensation, mixed with visions of Tegan, caused her to pull away quickly. A chill ran down her spine.

"Look!" one of the girls yelled.

Hair was creeping beneath the crack in the door. The girls sobbed and screamed. Rileigh covered her mouth with her hand. Tears fell down her cheeks.

Charlie was cold all over. *This is it. This is how you die.* Her hands tensed, clenched and unclenched, and brushed against something in her pocket. Her lighter.

She jerked it out and crouched down to the floor. The strands of hair seemed to sense her and rushed for her face. She flicked the flame on and thrust it at the hair.

An otherworldly scream erupted from the other side of the door as the locks shriveled and died beneath the flame. Tegan pulled away.

The room smelled like burning hair. Charlie gagged and covered her nose with her arm. She tried to listen for some kind of movement from the other side of the door. She could hear a faint dragging noise, but she couldn't pinpoint where it was.

She pressed herself against the cold linoleum and peered through the crack.

"Get up," Rileigh hissed, tugging at Charlie's shirt.

Charlie couldn't see anything. She sat up. "I need towels."

"Did you see it?" Tears were still falling down Rileigh's face, but her voice was strong and clear.

One of the girls pushed a pile of towels into Charlie's arms.

Charlie quickly bunched them up and pressed them beneath the crack.

"That's not going to stop it," the girl mumbled.

"Maybe it'll buy us a little time."

"A little time for what? We're going to die in here." Rileigh slumped onto the floor.

"We have to come up with a plan." Charlie paced.

"Can we at least get away from the door?" one of the girls asked.

Charlie helped Rileigh up and led her to the back of the locker room, where the girls sat, shaking and crying.

"There's no signal this far back," one of the girls sighed.

"Fuck."

"Did anyone try to call 911?" Rileigh asked.

"And tell them what? We're being attacked by a hair monster?"

"You could just tell them we need help. Tell them there was an accident." Rileigh swiped a phone from one of the girls and walked to the showers.

Charlie barely noticed. She was deep in thought, trying to think of something, anything, they could possibly do.

She only had the one lighter. She couldn't just stand there and burn the whole thing slowly. It would grab her. Her knees got weak at the thought of Amanda, laying on the floor with no scalp.

She went back to Rileigh's locker and pulled out the pack of cigarettes. Ten left. Maybe they could all light one and flick it onto Tegan. But would that even work? Would it catch quick enough? She didn't think so. But it was worth a shot at least.

She marched to the back and peeked into the locker room. Rileigh was slumped against the floor. She crouched beside her. "What's going on?"

"They're coming."

A wave of relief washed over Charlie. "Then we just have to survive until they get here. I have an idea."

Screams echoed off the tile.

Both girls jumped up. Rileigh gripped Charlie's arm. They exchanged a look. As quietly as they could manage, they crept toward the noise.

"Hide!" one of the girls cried. Feet slapped against the floor as the girls scattered.

Charlie peered around the corner. The towels were sliding across the floor, and almost like spilled ink, the hair pushed through after it.

Charlie pulled back and pressed herself against the tile. "Fuck. She's coming."

Out of her view Tegan crept along the floor, abandoning smaller pieces of hair in her wake. She poked into the rows of lockers one by one, looking for the girls, getting closer and closer.

Until she found one.

The girl's howls drowned out the pounding pulse in Charlie's ears.

"Get it off! Please help me! Help!"

"We've gotta get out of here." Rileigh was running before she'd even finished her sentence.

Charlie stared after her in shock, then managed to get her legs moving. The other girls were all bunched up together in the back row of lockers. "Come on!" Charlie motioned for them to follow her.

She looked down the rows as she ran, terrified of what she would see, but still needing to see it, needing to know.

She wished she hadn't.

A girl reached for Charlie as they passed one of the middle rows. She wasn't screaming anymore. She grabbed at her throat with her other hand as she wheezed. Charlie could see something black rolling in the back of the girl's mouth. Then slowly, she saw hair climb up the girl's eyes, turning the white to black.

And before she could pull away from her grip she began to expand, and her skin writhed, as though a million snakes had burrowed beneath her flesh and were trying to force their way out.

And then she exploded, showering Charlie in blood.

Charlie ran, wiping her skin frantically, hoping that no hair had landed on her. She swiped a towel off the floor as she ran.

The other girls were already on the other side of the pool, banging and pulling on the doors. Frantically, Charlie tried to ignite the towel as she ran, but it wasn't catching.

She came to a stop and tried again, starting at the tag. Finally, it took, and the flames marched lazily up the length of it. Charlie laughed.

"Charlie! Look out!" Rileigh was rushing toward her.

Before she could turn around, she was thrown to the floor. Tegan had swept her legs out from under her and was pulling herself up Charlie's legs.

Charlie threw the blanket on top of the mound of hair. It caught quicker than Charlie would have thought. Tegan screeched again. Charlie struggled to pull her legs out from beneath the burning mass, but it held fast to her legs, and began to pull her.

Charlie reached for the lighter she'd dropped in the impact, but was already too far away from it. She was dragging her to the pool.

"No!" Charlie screamed. If she could just manage to keep Tegan away from the pool for long enough, she would burn. She kicked her feet, but they didn't connect with anything, they simply sunk deeper into the hair.

Too late.

The two dropped into the water. Charlie used her long legs to push off the pool wall and propel herself away from Tegan. She didn't really know which way she was going, just that she had to get away. She kicked until her lungs felt like they would burst. When she finally surfaced, she found herself in the middle of the pool. But Tegan was still far at the other end, wading beneath the diving board.

Rileigh ran around the side of the pool to the ladder. "Over here!" She called.

Charlie began to kick her way over, but Rileigh's voice had stirred Tegan, and she was coming, impossibly fast.

Rileigh looked from Tegan to Charlie. She realized that Tegan would be on Charlie before she could get out. Or at the very least she'd catch her at the ladder and drag her back in. In the distance she could hear sirens, but they might be too late.

The other girls banged on the door and screamed, "In here! We're in here, please help!"

She rushed across the room to the supply closet and dragged out every chemical she could carry.

In the pool Charlie kicked as hard and as fast as she could. Her feet tingled, but when she looked back Tegan was still heading for her. Not far. Not far at all.

She reached out with her long arms and grazed the ladder as tears slid down her face. *So close.* She gripped the ladder with both hands.

This time the tickle she felt was real. Hair wrapped around her torso like fingers, pulling her away. But the hair, even drenched, didn't have much weight to it, so it began to climb up her instead.

Charlie wanted to scream, but she didn't want it to climb down her throat, so she closed her mouth tightly, pulling her lips between her teeth. She closed her eyes.

"Get back in the water!" Rileigh called from above her.

Charlie shook her head. Was Rileigh trying to kill her?

"Trust me."

Charlie hesitated, then took a deep breath through her nose and flopped back into the water.

Confused, Tegan released her.

Something was being thrown into the water. Charlie opened her eyes. Through the ripples she could see Rileigh dumping a powder into the pool. She threw the bucket in and started dumping a liquid next.

Charlie's skin itched and her eyes burned. She rose to the surface and coughed. She reached for her eyes; everything was turning black.

"Swim over here. Toward my voice." Rileigh chanted Charlie's name over and over as Charlie dragged herself through the water. All the while she could hear things hitting the water as Rileigh continued dumping the chemicals.

Charlie's itchy skin was replaced with an intense burn. She screamed. Her whole body ached.

"You're almost there! Don't stop."

Something made contact with the water, and it splashed into Charlie's mouth. She spat it out quickly, but the taste was acidic, and she could taste blood before long.

Finally, she gripped the ladder and began to drag herself up. Behind her she could hear Tegan gurgling and rolling around in the water.

Tendrils reached out for Charlie's legs, dragging her back. She dipped beneath the surface.

But the chemicals had already started to do their job, and the hair, now brittle and poisoned, began to break apart from the force.

Rileigh reached her hands in and pulled Charlie up. She helped her out and dragged her a few feet away from the pool, just in case.

Charlie rolled around on the ground, holding her burning skin, trying not to scream.

Tegan's screams split the room, drowning out the sound of the other girls' screams, drowning out the sound of the police finally breaking in.

Something splashed into Charlie's face. She gasped and tried to roll away, but her every movement was agony.

"It's ok, it's water. Open your eyes." Rileigh poured water from a bottle onto Charlie's face. Bottle after bottle.

Finally, Charlie could stand to open her eyes.

"Get out of the way," a man's voice commanded.

Rileigh disappeared from Charlie's view. She reached out for her.

"Don't leave me," she begged.

"It's ok. We're here," a woman answered. "We've got to get you out of here. You're covered in chemical burns."

They lifted her. Charlie watched chunks of her hair fall out from the movement. She whimpered.

"Is she dead?"

The paramedics hesitated. "Yes. She bled out."

"There's another one!" someone called from the locker room.

Charlie could hear the girls explaining to the police what had happened. She looked to the pool. The mound of hair was dissolving, sizzling and bubbling at the surface. She let her head drop back down.

"We're gonna get you some pain medicine when we get outside, ok?" the woman put herself into Charlie's line of vision.

Charlie reached up and felt her hair. It pulled apart like cotton candy.

Good. Tear it out. Tear it all out.

She watched the strands of hair on the floor as she was carried out. She could swear she saw them squirming.

ABOUT THE AUTHOR

KOURTNEA HOGAN is a horror hound from southern Indiana, transplanted to Pittsburgh. Raised on Stephen King novels and 80's horror movies, she fell in love with the genre at a young age and never looked back. She also writes scripts and makes her own movies after studying under George A. Romero.